SWEET MELODY

SHARON CORREIA

Sharon Correia xox

Love Was Every Time ♡

This one is for Cassie and Gela, the best coffee bitches a lady could ask for.

ONE

MELODY

"Please Melody. You know I wouldn't normally ask but I'm so sick. I'm scared that I might just throw up on the beautiful Logan Pierce if I do go and do this."

Standing in the hallway, I listen to my best friend, Avery begging me to go and fill in on her latest job. All whilst being stuck to the toilet.

Me and Avery share a house with her seven-year-old son, Zack. His piece of shit father up and left the second Avery told him that she was pregnant, so I stepped up and it's been just me, Avery, and Zack ever since. We moved to Salt Lake City around eighteen months ago as it was closer to where Avery was being offered jobs. Nothing was keeping us in Iowa, so we thought, why the heck not.

It just so happens to be my week off work, and I *was* planning on chilling out. Maybe even having a few days away to unwind, but given what is currently going down, I fear my plans are about to change.

"I don't know, Ree, this is way out of my comfort zone. They'll know straight away that I'm not you. I can't act."

Normally, I'd do anything for Avery, but I think this might just be a step too far. She's a model/actress and today she is supposed to be shooting a music video with the rock band, Guilty Pleasure. Whereas we do look a lot alike and have the same kind of build, I'm most definitely not a model and I'm certainly not an actress.

The biggest problem is, this job pays amazingly well, and money has been very tight around here lately. Avery turned her last job down at late notice as it meant going abroad for a whole month and leaving Zack with me. That in itself wasn't the problem, I'm always happy to have him. He's as much a part of my life as he is his mothers. The problem was the pay was very poor, she would have come back with very little money. So, she decided that it wasn't worth missing a month of her son's life for the sake of a few dollars. This job, however, is very well paid but as luck would have it, she has picked up a stomach bug from Zack.

"Oh please, Melody. You have run lines with me in the past and done a fab job. Anyway, you don't need to learn any lines for this. You just need to lie around and look all pretty and stuff."

The dry heave echoes around the bathroom as soon as she finishes her sentence.

Although some may disagree at this moment in time, Avery is stunning. She is the most naturally beautiful woman that I have ever met. She's a ten from the moment she opens her eyes in the morning. I'm lucky if I make it to a seven, and that's after I've spent hours in front of the mirror.

"That's different. That's just you and me, sitting around in our sweats, acting like complete dicks. This is going to be in front of people who are going to be watching me and judging me."

The thought of that makes my stomach roll and I panic for a

moment, praying that I haven't got what she has. Luckily it passes just as quickly as it came.

"Shut up, Melody, and stop doubting yourself. Just look at you. You're beautiful with your stunning figure, curves in just the right places, amazing auburn hair, and cute button nose. Don't even get me started on those eyes. Do you know I'd kill for my eyes to be the same shade of green as yours? Growing up, people always said we looked like twins, but I was always so jealous of your eyes. You are the best at everything you do, and if nothing else, just think of the money. This job will pay our rent for six months and still give us money to live."

How can I say no to that? No, really, how can I?!

"Okay, but you owe me. Big time."

This is where our weird relationship comes into play. She knows that I won't ask her for any money for doing this, but I know that she will pay the rent for the next six months and not ask me for any money towards it. It's very give and take with us, I will see that she and Zack are never without when she is in between jobs, and in return, she pays out as much as she can as soon as she has any money come in.

"OMG, I love you so much, Melody Grace. Or should I say, Miss Avery Moone?!"

———

I get all of the relevant information from Avery and before I know it, I am sitting in a car, on my way to the video shoot. Thankfully, the shoot is local and I'm still trying to get my head around what I have agreed to when we pull up to the location. I haven't had time to look through all the paperwork that she gave me before I arrived. Put that down to shock. The driver leads me into a warehouse that looks very, shall we say, rustic. As we step inside, everything changes. It's full of cameras and various sets for different scenes. My driver leads me through the set and straight to the back door where I'm greeted by a short man holding a clipboard.

"Hi, you must be Avery? If you'd like to follow me."

Almost correcting him about my name, I remember what I'm doing and who I'm doing it for.

"This will be the trailer that you'll be getting ready in. We did have separate trailers for the extras but as everyone else wrapped yesterday, we decided to return them all except for this one."

Feeling confused, I look at him as I tilt my head. I thought that this was an ongoing shoot. I really must look at the paperwork that Avery gave me.

We step into the trailer and it is beautiful. It's a lot larger than it looks on the outside.

"Make yourself comfortable as we've got a few more things to set up before we actually need you. Feel free to go through your wardrobe to make sure that everything is suitable and fits you as it should. Logan should be here at some point and you two can get to know each other a little bit better before we need you on set"

"Wait, what? Is this his trailer? Will I have to change with him watching? Because, apart from the postage stamp sized bathroom, I can't see anywhere else to go?"

He laughs at me. Short ass, clipboard man laughs at me.

"Oh honey, by the time the day is through, there probably won't be much of you that Logan hasn't seen"

With that, he turns and walks out. Leaving me alone in the trailer, more confused with each moment that passes.

Rather than standing around, dumbfounded, I decide to check out the wardrobe.

"What the fuck is this"

I'm practically screaming at the man who has just walked through the door, whilst shoving a nude thong and nipple covers in his face.

"Okay, darling, I'm here to calm you down a bit. I thought you might have an issue with some of the outfit choices. Have you actually read the script?"

Shit, I still haven't read the paperwork that Avery sent me with me. Looking up at him through my lashes, I feel my face flush as I offer him an apologetic smile.

I'm starting to doubt my ability as a stand-in for Avery when I can't even do something as simple as reading the script. Placing a comforting arm around me, he leads me to the nearest chair, guiding me down.

"Okay, darling, don't worry. Let's have a quick run through. The first thing that needs to be done is a real speedy photo shoot so that there are some pictures of the happy couple in their home. Then we move on to the fight scene. You just need to throw some shit around and scream a lot at your *boyfriend*."

He emphasizes the boyfriend using air quotes. Now that I've calmed down a bit, I realize just how gorgeous this man is. He's got to be over six-foot-tall, broad shoulders, beautiful blue eyes, dark hair that falls just past his shoulders, and the start of a beard that looks good on him. I don't normally like facial hair, but I think I'd make an exception for him.

"And then we move on to the scene where you will need that thong."

I can see his hesitation to tell me exactly what happens in that scene. To be honest, I think I'd rather not know.

Before he has a chance to continue, a small, slim man comes bursting through the door.

"Okay then, Hun, time to make sure your puss is camera ready"

"I beg your pardon? What the hell do you mean by that?"

"For the sex scene, Hun. I need to check that you're all shaved where I need you to be shaved. Nobody likes a hairy Mary."

I'm truly lost for words as he comes sauntering over to me

with a razor in one hand and shaving cream in the other. Just before he has the chance to grab me, I jump back

"Thank you for being willing to sort out my *Mary* for me but I will have you know that hairy Mary doesn't exist. My Mary has been hairless for years, so you won't be needed here, or down there, or anywhere else."

He huffs at me but then turns and makes his way out of the trailer as I sit on the edge of the makeshift bed behind me. Looking up into the baby blues of, whatever his name is, my shoulders sag in defeat.

"So, that's what you were so afraid to tell me then? I've got to get practically naked with some guy that I've never met. What the fuck have I got myself into. I can't believe I agreed to do this."

Tall, dark, and handsome comes and sits beside me as I feel like I'm about to cry.

"Come on, doll. You must've had some idea what you were getting into? Let me help you to relax and take your mind off it for a minute and then we can look at the script again, okay?"

I start nodding my head as his big hands grip my shoulders and start squeezing. Trying my hardest not to lose my shit, I decide the best thing to do is take his advice and not think about it for a minute. I'll just relax and enjoy this beautiful man's hands on me for as long as I can before I have to face my reality again.

TWO

MELODY

Five minutes later, and I am on the verge of losing my mind for a completely different reason. The moans that are coming out of my mouth are unnatural, but I swear I can't help it. This man knows exactly what he is doing. Feeling him move closer to me, he gently pulls my hair over to one side. His facial hair rubs on my neck as his lips gently touch my ear and he whispers. "People are gonna get the wrong idea about what exactly is going on in here with you making noises like that, doll."

As he talks, his lips gently caress my ear lobe. It's been so long since anyone has made me feel like this. Before I realize what I'm doing, I arch my head to the side, leaving my neck exposed. He takes his cue and starts kissing just below my ear whilst his hands work their way down my back, around my waist, and onto my stomach. He kisses me gently at first and then bites my earlobe. I inhale sharply at the sudden shock of pain. It didn't hurt, but it was an unexpected change in pace.

Hearing him snigger as one of his hands works its way up to my tit and he gives it a squeeze. He starts kissing my neck again, a little more passionately this time as his other hand works its way underneath my top. He takes a deep breath as his other hand reaches my tit and he confirms that I don't have a bra on. He gives it a firmer squeeze this time, tightening his fingers around my nipple. I let out a moan of pleasure which is greeted by another chuckle.

"Does that feel good, baby?" unable to form a proper sentence, I simply nod my head whilst biting down on my bottom lip.

Suddenly, he stops what he is doing and jumps out from behind me. Gasping in shock by his sudden movement, I look up to where he is now standing in front of me. He bends down, spreading my legs as he gets onto his knees. I try to say something but before the words come out, he puts his index finger to my lips.

"Shhhh, baby. Don't think, just feel."

Before I have a chance to think about what he's saying, his hands work their way up my thighs, under my skirt. Grabbing either side of my panties, he rips them down my legs and throws them over his shoulder. Kissing up my thigh, he makes his way closer and closer to the one place on my body that I've never let anyone put their mouth.

"Wow."

That's all I hear him say before he pushes me onto my back and spreads my legs apart a bit more. Everything in me wants to push back against him, not letting him see this very intimate part of myself but before I have a chance, his tongue gently strokes over my clit and I am instantly on the verge of an orgasm. He starts to apply a little more pressure, whist making circles around the tender spot. I didn't realize until now that I have my eyes closed, but curiosity gets the better of me as I open them and look down to see what he is doing. I'm greeted by his icy blue gaze staring back at me. He makes a visible play of stroking over my clit again, making sure this time that I see everything. My head falls back as I reach out and grab onto his hair, needing to touch him as the most intense orgasm of my life screams out of my body.

I'm still away with the fairies as I feel the bed dip next to me.

"That was fucking insane." looking over to him, I can see that his top is soaking wet.

"What's that? Did I pass out whilst you got a drink or something? It looks like you spilt it all over yourself."

The devilish smile that paints his face would be worthy of melting my panties off if I still had them on.

"Oh no baby, that was all you."

I have no clue what he is talking about, and he can tell by the look on my face.

"You squirted all over me. I mean, I've heard of this happening, I've even watched a few videos of it, but I've never had anyone squirt all over me before."

I. Am. Mortified.

Sitting up, I risk a look in between my legs. Sure enough, as well as everything that is on him, there is a wet patch on the bed and the floor. I attempt to get up, but he pulls me back down towards him.

"Don't run off baby, this is the hottest thing I have ever witnessed with my own eyes. I'm so fucking turned on right now, here." Grabbing my hand, he places it on the bulge in his jeans. Sure enough, he is hard. He is also fucking huge. I instinctively squeeze my hand around his cock. "Fuck!" he practically shouts, "I want to fuck you so bad, doll." The look of pure lust in his eyes right now is all it takes for me to start stroking up and down his beautifully long shaft. He practically leaps on me and starts kissing and biting my neck. Working his way down to my tits, whilst pushing my top up, he grazes my nipple with his teeth. After what he has just done to my body, I wouldn't think that I would be able to feel anything from the waist down for a while, but I was wrong. It's like my nipple has a direct line to my pussy every time he touches it. Lifting himself up a bit, he makes light work of pushing his jeans and boxers down enough to free himself. He lifts my leg and places it round his waist. Feeling his dick push against my entrance, I've never wanted anyone as much as I do at this moment. He looks me in the eyes as if asking permission, so I look down and give a gentle nod, to reassure him. With that, he thrusts into me so hard and fast that I swear he has torn me in two. Unable to hold in the small squeal that leaves my mouth, he freezes.

"Oh god, baby, you're so fucking tight. Are you okay?"

Nodding, I feel the pain ease as I finally utter the words he is waiting to hear,

"I'm okay."

Looking up at him I can see the desperation in his eyes, as he smiles down at me, the strain evident on his face. His mouth finally meets with mine and he gently kisses me, as he starts to make slow, careful movements with his hips. And just like that, the pain disappears. I never knew that the simplest of movements could feel so amazing, feeling nothing but him, filling me in a way I've never known. Speeding up the movement of his hips, it doesn't take long before he's thrusting into me with a fierce, intense passion. He starts biting at my neck again and the pain of it, mixed with the pleasure he is creating between my legs has me teetering on the brink of another orgasm. "Baby, you feel so good, I'm gonna cum."

That's all it takes to push me over the edge as we both explode, feeling him fill me up in a way I have never experienced before, and at this moment in time, I don't care. No man has ever made me feel the things he just has, and in a short space of time too.

We lay there for what feels like an age, with him still inside of me as we hear a knock on the door.

"Miss Avery, I'm here to do your hair. Is it okay to come in, babe?"

"No!" we both yell in unison as he removes himself from me and pulls his jeans back into place. Noticing the emptiness I feel inside of me as soon as he does, I do my best to shake it off and straighten myself up. Scrambling around, I find my panties on the dresser of all places. He must have thrown them over there whilst I was otherwise occupied. Putting them back on as quickly as possible, I shimmy my skirt back into place. Shuffling his way over to me, he smirks whilst looking at my neck.

"Sorry doll, I think I got a bit carried away." Lifting his hand, he gently strokes over the place his eyes are focused on, before he leans in and gives it a little kiss. As he pulls away, we both stop for a moment and look into each other's eyes. The bang at the door destroys the moment as his hand drops from my neck. Turning away, I sit down at the dressing table as he makes his way to the door. It's at that exact moment when I realize that I don't even know his name. Opening the door, he gestures for the hairstylist to come in. They nod at each other as the stylist blurts out.

"Oh, Logan. I wasn't expecting it to be you. The noises coming out of here made me think that it was Cody or Hunter. Or even both." She giggles and winks. Letting me know this isn't her first time working with them. As I finally realize what she said, my mouth runs away from me.

"Logan? As in, Logan Pierce?"

He smiles the biggest smile I've seen yet,

"Yes doll, the one and only. See you on set."

With that, he exits the trailer. But not before giving us a wink that has both me and the hairstylist blushing. Leaving me totally and utterly speechless.

Hair and makeup all happen in a blur, thank goodness. The

hairstylist was the ultimate professional and not once did she make me feel uncomfortable. In fact, she helped me to clean up the mess that was left behind from my new found bodily function. I was so ashamed at that moment but she made me feel loads better with a joke about motorboating. If I hadn't been so mortified, it would have been hilarious, but a fantastic ice breaker, nonetheless.

My head is still in a spin as I'm ushered onto the set. Thankfully, for this first scene, I am fully dressed. The director makes his way over to me, I know it's the main guy because he is wearing a sweater that has the word **director** written across the front.

"Alright babe, are you ready? I need to get through this as quickly as we possibly can as we don't have much time left. Now, just loosen up a little and act natural, Logan's a good guy, you're in safe hands with him." He winks at me and makes his way over to Logan. Without even realizing that I have done it, I raise my hand to my neck and stroke the area that Logan was biting earlier. Quickly removing it before I smudge the makeup that was needed to cover it. Logan saunters over and holds out his hand.

"Hey, I'm Logan. I'm the man that you will be fucking later." I don't know what to say but I feel my cheeks getting redder and redder. Placing my hand in his, I whisper.

"Are you serious? After what just happened. Maybe it might have helped if you had actually introduced yourself before that."

"Come on, doll, you must have known who I was?" The smug look on his face has my cheeks flushing with anger this time.

"I hate to break this to you, Logan, but I really didn't have a clue. I hadn't even heard about your band until this all got dumped on me this morning."

Realizing my mistake, I stutter whilst trying to think of something to say, to make this okay.

"I thought they sent out the paperwork a week ago? Why did you only see it this morning, Avery? God, you really are unprepared if you didn't bother looking at it until today. That makes sense though, because if you had looked, you would have seen that we have a bedroom scene to shoot after this. It's a good job for you that I haven't got time to look for somebody else now."

With what he just said, I start to feel a bit braver, so I decide it's time to tell him the truth.

"Logan, you said you won't fire me, right?" Before he has the chance to answer, the director starts screaming for us to get on set. Logan looks at me questionably, and I realize that now is not the time to tell him. So, I shrug my shoulders as I make my way over to the set. Hopefully, I can just get on and get this done before I make more of a fool of myself. What's the point in telling him anyway? It won't lead to anything. He probably has women falling at his feet with each flash of his pearly whites.

We fly through a lot of the scenes quickly, I wasn't sure if we would click after what just happened, but we're getting on great. We even manage to make each other laugh at the most inappropriate times. The fight scene is my favorite so far. Throwing loads of stuff at him, including food, whilst we screamed shit at each other. We did get told off by the director a few times as we were laughing when we should have been angry, but we managed to muddle our way through. Now though, comes the scene that I've been dreading. They saved it for last, at Logan's request, so that we could have a closed set. I'd like to think that he did this because he knows how freaked out I am about the lack of clothes but honestly, I'm not sure. Whatever his reasons, I'm very grateful. Putting on the thong and nipple covers, as well as a dressing gown, I make my way back onto the set. The hairstylist, once again, calmed my nerves and made me feel a bit more at ease with what's about to happen. She also pointed out that Logan has already seen everything, so I don't have to worry about that. I probably would have slapped her if it wasn't true. Logan hasn't come back to the trailer at all since this morning, but I've been told that he's ready and waiting.

The set is stunning. A huge king-size bed is placed in the middle with white sheets covering it. All around the bed are white curtains with wind machines around them. Looking up, I see Logan enter the makeshift bedroom wearing nothing but a pair of nude, tight-fitting boxers. He is breathtaking. I never got to see the whole package earlier, so I make sure to take my time and appreciate it now. The first thing that stands out is his broad shoulders and chest. He has the working of a six-pack and the most beautiful tanned skin. I can't help but squeeze my thighs together as I take it all in. Finally, I work my eyes upwards to look at his handsome face, that's when I notice that he's staring at me too.

Walking over, he takes my hand and leads me to the bed.

"Are you ready for this, doll?"

I can only nod as I seem to have lost the ability to speak once more. Stopping at the side of the bed and standing in front of me, he starts to undo my dressing gown. Slowly pushing it from my shoulders so it falls to the floor in a heap. He pulls back the sheet and guides me into the bed. Unable to take my eyes off him, he's so mysterious and sexy as sin. What I'd give right now to know what is going on in that gorgeous head of his as he shuffles into bed next to me.

The moment is interrupted as the director shouts.

"Right then people, let's get this over and done with so that we can all go home. Logan, would you please mount the lovely lady and make it appear as if you love each other. I want to see lots of kissing and dry humping going on, okay?"

"Yes boss," is all Logan says as he pushes me back onto the pillows and works his way on top of me.

"You're gonna feel my dick poking you, doll, but I'm not

gonna apologize for it, not when it's your fault anyway. I mean, who comes onto a video shoot wearing nothing but a thong?"

Letting out a laugh at his silly comment, I see him laughing too whilst staring at me with those sinful eyes again. He pulls a sheet over us and kisses me on the forehead as the director yells,

"ACTION!"

THREE

MELODY

E verything moves slowly at first. The fans all fire up, blowing the curtains around. The noise from the fans and the music playing rattles around my ears as I try to get my head in the game. Logan buries his head in my neck, making out like he is kissing it and I try to look like I'm enjoying it, all the while trying not to look at the cameras that are pointed at us. This carries on for another few minutes and then we hear the director yell

"CUT."

Stomping over to us, he bellows.

"What the fuck are you two doing? You're supposed to be madly in love, but you look like an old married couple who have decided to have sex because there isn't anything better to do. You're a young, hot couple who are about to have some crazy sex, can you start showing it please. Jesus Christ Logan, fuck her like you mean it, yeah?"

He stomps back off before either of us has a chance to answer.

"AND ACTION".

"Do you trust me, doll?"

Logan whispers whilst the director is screaming. Choosing to put my faith in him, I nod, not knowing what he's got planned.

Grabbing my leg, he lifts it around his waist. He was right, I can feel his dick poking me in my pussy. My head instinctively falls back as I open my mouth but before any noise escapes, his lips cover mine. His tongue invades my mouth, and we enter into what seems like a battle for supremacy. Our tongues are at war as his hand grabs hold of my thigh and squeezes, hard. He starts moving his hips and the friction against my clit is sublime. I try to cry out, but he just swallows my cries and carries on kissing me. His hand slowly makes its way up to my waist and before I can stop it, he grabs my tit. This time, he is the one to moan out loud before I can swallow it down. I do however manage to bite on his bottom lip gently as his lips escape mine.

Right then, he looks directly into my eyes. The moment is so intense that words aren't needed. His hand comes up to my cheek and he gently strokes it.

Smiling just a little as he moves his hand down and squeezes it around my throat. Applying a small amount of pressure as he continues to kiss everywhere that his hand isn't touching on my neck. Slowly, he makes his way down to my collar bone, all the while grinding his hips and creating that breath-taking friction as his dick pushes against my clit. Removing his hand from my throat, he strokes me all the way down to my hip. I am on the edge right now and he knows it. He looks me in the eye and smirks but before I can react, he presses his lips to mine. It's right at that moment that a toe-curling orgasm rips its way out of my body. Logan swallows my screams once more as he kisses me.

Feeling myself come back down to earth as the director yells cut. I can't believe that this happened. I've just had an orgasm whilst being watched. Not only watched though, recorded for a fucking music video. I will never be able to escape this.

Finally, I decide to open my eyes and that's when I notice that Logan is stroking my hair.

"Hey doll, you okay?"

I nod, again, as I can't seem to form any words, *again*. This man is so gorgeous, I don't think that I could ever get bored of looking at him. Just as I go to talk, the director interrupts us.

"Guys that was amazing. I think that's a wrap. I was gonna do some other positions, but I don't think we'll get better than that."

Logan nods at him as he turns and walks away.

"Can someone please grab us both a dressing gown, I wouldn't want to embarrass anyone with this big fucking hard on I'm currently sporting." My cheeks flush once more as he looks down at me, laughing. Not able to hide my embarrassment, I grimace as I look up at him.

Why would he shout that out to everyone?

As I am thinking that, he leans down and whispers in my ear.

"Don't worry, doll, I haven't got a hard on. I just shot my load with you and I don't want to embarrass either one of us with the mess that is most definitely down there."

He lifts his body off mine and we both look down. He's right, it is a fucking mess. There is no way that we could hide that from anyone if he were to get up. We both start to laugh uncontrollably as someone drops two dressing gowns on the bed next to us. As I look around, everyone who is left on set is starting to walk away. It's at that moment that Logan leaps up and puts on the dressing gown before anyone sees, so I follow suit. Deciding not to hang around, I make my way to the trailer. Within five minutes, I'm in, dressed, and back out. The man that brought me here this morning is waiting outside the door as I open it.

"I'm here to take you back home Miss Moone." Following

him to the car, I get in before I make a fool of myself some more. I could have tracked down Logan and gave him my number but let's be fair, he is a world-famous rock star who probably gets up to this kind of thing on a daily basis. If he wants me that badly, he'll know how to get hold of me. or Avery should I say. The director and producer both have her number and I'm sure he has the means to find it if he wants it that bad. Just because he is the first man to ever have his head between my legs and elicit that type of reaction from me, doesn't mean he will even remember my name by the morning. Let alone want my number. Even if he does remember my name, that's the other problem. It's not actually my name. Not a good basis to try and start a relationship, is it? I get in the car and go home before anything else crazy happens today.

FOUR

LOGAN

I fucked up. I'm not the kinda guy who fucks just anybody, but there was a strange innocence about Avery that instantly drew me in and had me doing things I should never have done. It was wrong of me not to tell her who I was straight away, but it made a change not to be recognized. I wasn't a hundred percent convinced that she didn't recognize me but the look on her face when I finally told her who I was, was the type of thing that you can't fake. In this business, I'm surrounded by fakes. You learn pretty quickly how to spot them. I mean, you have to, otherwise they would eat you alive.

I feel awful though, like I just used her innocence to help cleanse my dirty soul. You could say, considering she opened her legs to me that quickly, that she wasn't as innocent as I felt she was, but the look on her face when I went down on her and she squirted everywhere. That was one of the most beautiful things I have ever seen, helped very much by the fact that she tasted fucking incredible. I could happily feast on her every day if things were different. I overstepped the mark enough by sticking

20

my dick in her but what I did to her on set was unforgivable. Absolutely out of this world but unforgivable nonetheless and the best/worst thing about this is the fact that I have to watch it over and over again as me and the guys sit down and help put the video together. It's unusual to start editing the next day but we need to move this one as quickly as we can. Having just got back from quite an intense tour, it's best to strike whilst the iron is hot and remind everyone sitting at home just who the fuck we are.

I hope that the other guys don't notice how intense and real things were.

Our producer is the first one here, and he starts setting everything up straight away. Cody, our lead guitarist, and Spencer, our rhythm guitarist, are the next to arrive, arguing over something. These guys argue all the time, but it rarely turns serious. I think that Cody still struggles with Spencer's dry sense of humor. Spencer is English, along with Eddie, our bassist and their sense of humor is very dry and sarcastic. Even though we've all known each other for many years, Cody still struggles to get his head around it and it ends up with him losing his temper with Spencer every time. Eddie, who has just arrived, is the quiet one. He has the same English humor, but he tends to keep to himself a lot more. He never gives much away about himself or any of his family, but he is also the first to say if you have pissed him off, although he does have the most patience out of all of us. If it wasn't for Eddie, this band would have been done years ago. I don't know the whole story, because he keeps it all to himself, but he inherited a lot of money when he turned twenty-one and he invested a huge amount of it into the band. He also shot a lot of it into his arm. He's been clean for a while now but we all still worry about him falling off the wagon. Heroin is a horrific thing and it's also something that isn't easy to give up, but he seems to be doing okay, so far. Last to arrive, as always is our drummer, Hunter.

"Hey fuckers, let's get this shit done then. What are we all waiting for?" We all throw something at him, and I shoot back.

"Shut your mouth, shit for brains. Next time we're starting without you." I always tell him that, as he always seems to be late but he never fucking listens. But then again, we never start without him.

Dan, our producer, seems to have done most of the work already, so he shows us what he has put together so far. The scenes of me and Avery in the bedroom are making me rock fucking hard. She looks amazing and Dan has happened to use a shot of her when I know she was mid-orgasm. The memory of it nearly has me shooting my load again, right here in a room full of men.

We watch and edit for a few hours until I can't take any more, so I excuse myself and head to the bathroom. The relief I feel as soon as I get in that cubicle and have my dick in my hand is unbelievable. The images of Avery and me, in that bed, remembering what she sounded like when she orgasmed has me blowing my load in no time at all. I can't remember the last time a woman had this kind of effect on me. Well, that's not strictly true. Right now, I'm feeling like a fucking teenager again, having to have a sneaky wank just to get some relief. I clean up and make my way back into the editing room, ignoring the guilt that claws away at me.

"Fucking hell Logan, were you actually fucking this girl? That is the most realistic sex scene that I've ever seen outside of porn. The chemistry between you two is un-fucking-believable. I hope you got her number?" Hunter looks at me, waiting for an answer that he isn't going to get.

"Shut the fuck up H. Some of us can actually be near a girl without having to stick our dick in it, you know." I say the words, knowing in this instance that wasn't the case. Hunter shrugs his shoulders and walks back to his chair muttering something that I didn't quite catch. The look on everyone's face is the same as Hunter's, letting me know that they are all thinking it too.

I take a seat next to Eddie, he's the one least likely to give me shit about the whole thing.

We finish the editing a few hours later and I can honestly say that I am hugely impressed with the results. Me and Avery really do seem to have good chemistry on screen, well, it wasn't just on-screen but that's all I'm willing to admit right now. Cody, Hunter, and Spencer shoot out the door as soon as possible but Eddie lingers behind. Knowing him the way I do, I know he wants to say something because he is usually the first to leave. Although before, he'd be running off to his dealer because he knew that we wouldn't tolerate being with him when he was high. Hearing him take a deep breath, I brace myself for what's to come.

"Logan, you know I don't normally get involved in any of the shit that goes on behind the scenes but even I could see the chemistry between you and that chick. I don't know if you did fuck her and, being honest, I don't want to know. All I'm gonna say is, you need to keep your head straight. And we both know I'm not talking about your dick. You've got a lot of shit going on at home and the last thing you need is to get your head fucked up by some girl." He's right. I need to put her out of my head and move on. I can't get involved with anyone right now, the timing couldn't be any worse.

"Thanks man." That's all I manage to say to him as we shake hands. Leaving me with nothing but my fucked-up head.

FIVE

MELODY

Days pass by as if nothing ever happened. I still haven't told Avery what went on between me and Logan because honestly, I'm too embarrassed. My only hope is that I haven't done any damage to her career or given her the wrong kind of reputation. I've never been so thankful that Avery is ill right now in my whole life. Dodging her and avoiding her constant questions about Logan would have been a lot harder had she been okay.

The sun is shining bright, so I decide to take Zach to the park. With his Mom feeling off, the poor boy has been stuck inside for days now.

The park is packed, as I expected but Zack instantly spots his best friend Ozzy and goes running over to him. Ozzy and Zack have been inseparable since the day they met and often, they will have sleepovers either with us or over at Ozzy's house. His Mom is amazing. She's married but we've never met the husband. She says that he works away a lot, but he spends as much time as he can with his son. We did wonder for a while if he was in the military but even soldiers get to come home sometimes.

We often get together with Gabriella, Ozzy's Mom, when the kids have sleepovers as it gives us all a chance to unwind whilst the kids burn off some energy. We've been to her house on numerous occasions now and the strangest thing is, she doesn't have any pictures of her husband anywhere. Sure, there are loads of pictures of Ozzy and even a few of her and Ozzy but none of the husband.

Another one of mine and Avery's crazy theories was that maybe he worked for MI5 and that's why she couldn't have any pictures of him around. She often changes the subject if we ever mention him, distracting us with another glass of wine. Moving to Utah, we discovered that a lot of people who live here are Mormons, Gabby included. We had another notion that maybe the husband left but she didn't want to risk any backlash from the church, so they kept it quiet. She may like to have a drink now and again, but we have learned over time that she takes her religion very seriously, going to church every chance she gets. Being a single Mom is not an option in her eyes, we know that much. We also know she holds nothing against Avery for being a single Mom, it's just not the life she wants for herself. Either way, we don't care as long as our friend is happy. Which she must be as her son is a shining light everyone needs.

Making my way over to the edge of the park, I watch Zach and Ozzy run circles around the slide, running up the steps and sliding down. I don't know where they get their energy from, I'm exhausted just watching them. Smiling at Zach as he looks my way, that's when Ozzy spots me. He comes running over to me, as fast as his little legs can take him, and jumps straight into my open arms.

"Dee dee I missed you. Can I come over for dinner? Pretty please? With a cherry on top."

This boy is just too irresistible for words. I start making my way over to where his Mom usually sits, with him still in my arms and Zack running off ahead.

"I'll need to speak to your Mom, little dude, to make sure that she hasn't got any other plans."

"No, Dee dee, it's okay……"

"No, little dude, it's not okay, you know I need to ask your mo…"

"What the fuck are you doing with my son?" Hearing a voice I vaguely recognize, I turn to where it emanated from.

"Put him the fuck down before I call the police."

My mouth drops open when I see Logan looking back at me with rage in his eyes. It takes me a moment to realize those words that came from him, are actually directed at me. Staring down at Ozzy, in my arms, the penny finally drops that he *is* talking to me, telling me to put *his* son down. Placing Ozzy down, I look to Logan not knowing what to say.

"I didn't know that he was your son," I stutter, as he runs over to his Dad saying

"It's okay, Daddy, this is Dee…" Cutting Ozzy off before he has the chance to finish his sentence, Logan shoots daggers at me as he hisses.

"We need to go now, son. This lady is obviously crazy and has decided to stalk me. This isn't okay, Avery. If I see you again, I will phone the police. Do I make myself clear?"

"No Daddy, she isn't Avery, she's Dee dee."

Logan has a confused look on his face, so I take this moment to try and talk to him.

"Logan look, I was dishonest with you the other day, I'm not Avery. My name is Melody. Avery is my friend who I live with, she's Zack's Mom and it was supposed to be her that was filming with you, but she got sick and couldn't leave the house. We've never done this before, but I couldn't let her lose that amount of money, not with Zack to think of and…"

"Just stop Avery. Or Melody, or whoever the fuck you are.

I've got too much going on right now for me to be caught up in this bullshit. I've got to take Ozzy to the hospital for his Mom's appointment. I don't want to, but shit happens. I haven't got time for this as well."

"Hospital appointment? Is everything okay? I panic. "Do you need me to have Ozzy? He's always welcome at our place."

By the time I notice just how angry Logan is, it's too late. The words erupt from him.

"Just leave us alone and stay the fuck away from me and my family. Do I make myself clear?"

With that he turns and walks away, taking a very unhappy boy and leaving me more confused than ever. I manage to hold back the tears as Zach jumps into my arms, looking sad about what just transpired.

I feel everyone's eyes on me, and it lets me know that now is a good time for us to leave. For a busy park, it's gone awfully quiet.

On my way back to the car, my boss calls me asking if I can go back to work a few days early. Normally, I'd probably keep him hanging for a bit but one of the staff has walked out and left him short. With everything that has gone on the past couple of days I honestly think I could do with the distraction. I agree to go back before the standard begging and hang up before he has a chance to question me. He knows I'm a pushover when it comes to him, but I usually make him work for it first.

I take Zach home and hope to god that he doesn't say anything about what happened today to his mother. I can barely get my head around all of this, let alone try and explain it all to Avery. I know I'm gonna have to tell her soon, but I'm nowhere near ready for that yet. Not whilst I'm still so confused. Is he really Gabriella's husband? The guy that me and Avery have been so curious about? The guilt I feel even thinking that he could be, eats me up inside.

Thankfully, she doesn't have a chance to talk to me as I hurry in, telling her I have to go to work. Rushing to my room, I get ready at lightning speed and go running out of the door as fast as my legs can carry me. The drive to the club isn't long but it is long enough to have a good cry to myself. The implications of what I have done are slowly starting to sink in. It's at this moment that I am highly thankful to be working tonight as I pull into the parking lot.

Making my way towards the club, I see that the lights in the sign are flickering again, so I give the electrical box a whack and that seems to do the trick. Most people would be ashamed to admit that they work in a place like this but not me. Working in a strip club wasn't something I saw myself doing when I was younger, but here I am.

I'm not one of the dancers. Not because I think it's something to be ashamed of because I have mad respect for the ladies who do it. But because I can't dance for shit, but I do pour a mean whisky sour.

The uniform is minimal. Short black shorts, and a low-cut black top with the club logo on the back, the club's name on the front as well as a name tag—as the boss wants everyone to be called by name. It took me a minute to get used to the uniform as it does show a bit more skin than I like but now that I've got used to it, I wouldn't want any different. I choose to pair it up with some flat, knee-high boots because you're on your feet the whole shift. So, they make me feel sexy but comfortable.

"Well hello, Miss Melody, how kind of you to *grace* us with your presence. Did you see what I did there?!"

This was funny the first time I heard it, but I've known Barry, my boss, ever since I can remember. He's an old family friend who has been saying the same thing to me my whole life. "Very funny Barry. How are you not married off yet?" This is the only thing that I can say to get Barry to back down. If I didn't say it, he would be on one all night. Don't get me wrong, Barry doesn't want a wife and kids, but he still doesn't like anyone pointing it out to him.

Winking at him, I blow him a kiss as I walk by on my way to the staff room to put my bag away. It looks busy out there tonight which is a very good thing as it has been slowing down a bit of late. Over the past few months, sales have been down, and we've even had to let some of the girls go. I'm privy to this information as I help Barry with his record-keeping. He is the most unorganized person I have ever met. He hasn't officially promoted me to manager or assistant manager yet, but he makes sure that I am compensated financially for everything I do. I make my way to the bar, grabbing my pad and pen so that I'm good to go. Just before I make my way out onto the floor Barry shouts over to me.

"Looks good in here tonight Dee, let's hope this is the way forward" He smiles as I make my way to the club floor.

It's been busy enough tonight to take my mind off the fucked-up situation I've found myself in, but I know it still isn't enough for the club. Considering it's a Friday night, we should've been rushed off our feet, but I think it's fair to say this wasn't the case. I didn't stop all night, but it wasn't the crazy chaos that I had grown used to. But on the plus side, at least it's picking up a bit. A few more weekends like that and things will be fine. I stay behind and help Barry do the cleaning and cashing up.

"Not bad tonight, eh, Bazza?" He has a sad smile on his face because he knows as well as I do that one fairly good night is not enough.

"It wasn't a bad night, but it wasn't a great night either, Dee dee. We just need an injection of cash and I can make things good again. I can re-open the rooms that need fixing and hire some more girls, but with what I have right now, it's not gonna happen. I haven't got enough girls for the clients, so they just end up going elsewhere. I don't wanna moan and go on Dee but you're the only person I can vent to. I appreciate you going behind my back to try and get a loan but I'm happy they said no. I don't want you being lumbered with my debt. If I ever find out about you doing anything like that again, I will fire your ass." Barry smiles as he leans over to hug me. It's true, I went behind Barry's back to try and get a loan to help him out, but the bank said no as I didn't have anything to use as collateral. He wouldn't have ever found out either if it wasn't for Avery coming in one night, getting blind drunk, and telling him all about it.

"You know I'd do anything for you Barry. I love you like a *way* older brother." We both laugh as we finish cashing up for the night.

SIX

MELODY

The rest of the weekend was the same at work, busy enough to keep you moving but not enough to turn a decent profit. Barry has given me today and tomorrow off as he interrupted the last few days of my holiday. So, I decide to use the voucher that Avery got me as a thank you gift for covering her ass last week, for an all-expenses-paid spa day. It even includes a cut and blow-dry at the spa's salon. Avery is around to sort out Zack, thanks to the money from the music video, so I leave her a note and head out for the day, with my phone on silent.

By the time I leave the spa, I am so relaxed I'm convinced that my bones are made out of jelly. I should go out and show off my radiant skin and new hairdo but I'm worried that I may fall asleep at any moment. Everything is quiet when I arrive home, so I decide not to disturb Avery and just go to bed. I rummage through my bag to find my phone so that I can take a quick selfie whilst my hair still looks good. No doubt I won't be able to get it looking like this again. I notice a missed call from a number I don't recognize and a message letting me know I have a voicemail. It's late so I decide it can wait till the morning. I'm sure If it was that important whoever it was would've tried calling more than once. As soon as I've finished getting ready for bed, I place my phone on the charger and the moment my head hits the pillow, I am out like a light.

I wake up to Zack, sitting on my bed.

"Wake up, sleepy head. I missed you yesterday. Can you take me to the park? please?" Avery comes crashing through the door and gives Zack 'the look'.

"I told you Zachary to leave Melody alone. It's her day off and it was rude of you to disturb her. Now go to your room, like I asked you please."

"But Mom…"

"But Mom nothing, young man. Say sorry to Melody and go to your room, now."

Zach looks as if he is about to cry but I know that I can't go against what his mother said, so I give him a squeeze and he jumps off the bed.

"Sorry Dee dee." My heart almost breaks for him. He has the saddest look on his face that I've ever seen. Waiting for him to leave the room, I turn to Avery.

"If you haven't got any plans today then I would like to take him to the park. I feel like I haven't spent any time with him." I didn't mean to say the park, but the words were out before I remembered what happened the other day. Avery smiles at me because she knows that I'm not even a little bit mad at Zach for waking me up.

"Only if you're sure. I haven't made any plans, but I do need to do a grocery shop and it's so much easier when he's not with me."

"It's settled then, I will take Zach to the park and you will feed us all later. Shall I take a picnic with us? It doesn't matter if we stay out later than planned then." Avery nods.

"Good idea, I'll go and get everything ready for you whilst you sort yourself out"

Avery shuts the door behind her as she leaves. Picking up my phone to check the time, I see the voicemail message I ignored last night, so I give it a listen now.

"Hey Melody, it's Logan. Look, I'm really sorry about the other day. Ozzy has been pestering me to sort this all out as he misses Zach and we were wondering if you'd like to meet us in the park tomorrow for lunch?"

Tomorrow is today, shit. Hitting redial on the number I don't recognize, I try not to overthink it before I change my mind. As soon as it rings, I realize that this is a bad idea and pull my phone away from my ear, ready to hang up.

"Hey Melody," I hear at a distance and realize that it's too late.

"Hi Logan."

"I thought I wasn't gonna hear from you." It feels strange to hear him calling me by my name and not Avery's.

"Ummm… How did you get my number?"

"Oh, yeah, your number was on the emergency contacts list. I hope you don't mind?"

"No, I don't mind. Aren't you a bit worried though? I mean, now that I have your number, my stalking could go up another level." He laughs quietly and I carry on talking before things become awkward.

"Honestly, Logan, it's fine. Me and Zach were already planning on going to the park anyway so it would be awesome if Ozzy was there too."

"Okay, shall we say around twelve?"

"Twelve is good, I'll make sure that I have enough food for Ozzy. Are you sure you're okay being seen with your crazy stalker though?"

Logan sees the funny side of my question as he laughs out loud down the phone.

"Okay funny girl. We'll be there for Twelve. If you're lucky, I might even say hi this time instead of just balling you out." He lets out another small laugh as he hangs up. What a prick. Right now, I'm not sure if I like him or loathe him. Looking at the time on my phone, I see it's already 11am. I can't believe that I slept for so long. Jumping out of bed, I have the fastest shower of my life and then make myself as presentable as possible. I haven't got time to do a full face of makeup so I just dust over my face with some powder foundation and apply a bit of lip gloss. Zach is driving his mother insane by the time I'm ready, so I grab the picnic basket that Avery prepared, being sure to throw in a few extra bits for Ozzy.

"You look nice, Dee. That spa day seems to have done you the world of good. Fingers crossed for a D.I.L.F. at the park." Avery nudges my shoulder as I pick the basket off the counter. Trouble is, there is going to be a Dad there that I've already fuc... I banish away that thought before my cheeks turn a crimson shade of red.

Parking the car, I take out Zach, being sure to grab the picnic basket as we make our way down to the park. I know the exact moment Zach spots Ozzy as he lets out an almighty squeal and goes running in his direction. Judging by the way they embrace each other I think it's safe to say they've missed one another a lot. I see Logan standing on the other side of the park, watching the boys so I make my way over to him.

"Hey. Is it okay to be standing this close to you or has the restraining order kicked in?" I can't help but laugh before I finish my sentence. He sees the funny side and laughs with me,

"Ahhh funny girl. It's good to see you. I really am sorry about the other day." Turning towards me, I can see the sincerity in his face, "I hope you understand, just a little bit. Ironically, you're not my first stalker. I know it's not an excuse but I'm on my guard when it comes to my boy."

I didn't know that he had had a stalker in the past. Although, I didn't know who he was until recently, so why would I? This makes things a lot more understandable though. Still, I'm not going to make it that easy for him.

"To be fair, I have been told in the past that I am a bit stalkerish. But being honest, I don't think you're the type of guy I would stalk. I mean, you're no Jared Leto." seeing his jaw drop in the corner of my eye, I refuse to make eye contact with him, but I can see the unamused look on his face.

"You're right there, doll, I ain't no Jared Leto. I'm Logan mother fucking Pierce and don't you forget it."

As my eyes finally reach his, I turn myself around fully so that I am face to face with him.

"Do you always have such a potty mouth, Logan mother fucking Pierce? Or do you save that especially for me?" Logan chuckles to himself as he bites his bottom lip. I don't think that I have ever found someone biting their lip so sexual before. I swear to all that is holy that this man could make anything look sexy. Shaking my head, I start setting up the picnic before I end up standing there staring at him the whole time. He helps me lay out the blanket and we both sit down at the same time. I notice that Logan starts unloading some of the food from his picnic basket just as the kids come running over. Zach takes a seat next to me as Ozzy runs up to me and gives me a huge hug.

"Daddy, I soooo hungry. Can we eat now, please?" This kid is the best. The angelic look on his face would make the strongest of soul's wobble.

"Yes son, take a seat. Me and Melody will sort you both out some food."

The kids fill their faces and go back over to the play area.

After a few minutes of silence and awkward glances, I try and think of something, anything to say.

"So, tell me about what it's like to tour? Are you still local or have you branched out yet?" The question seems to catch Logan off guard as he throws me an amused look.

"Still local? Is this another one of your jokes?" Confused, I offer him a shrug of the shoulders. "It has it's good points and bad points. I love connecting with the fans, but I miss my boy when I'm gone. It can be hard work at times, especially with Cody, Hunter and Spencer constantly looking to get their dicks wet, whereas me and Eddie just want the quieter life. We aren't interested in that side of fame." I blush slightly as he looks over to me, remembering a side of him that I never had the right to see.

"Logan, I think…"

"Just give me time, okay? I know what you're gonna say and I promise you, you will have answers. I just can't give them to you right now. You're gonna have to trust me, okay, doll?" I don't know what it is about him that makes me want to trust him, but I do.

"Okay, I trust you. I'm also sorry about the whole mess me and Avery created. I should never have agreed to go on that video shoot and pretend to be her."

He leans over and places his hand on my knee.

"It's okay, Melody, with what Ozzy has said over the past

few days, I think I've figured it out. Let's just forget everything and start over." He removes his hand and starts packing up. I can't say that that didn't hurt, just a little bit. As I don't think I'll ever forget what happened that day.

"Oh, and Melody." I look up into his big blue eyes. "I never thought that Avery suited you anyway. I much prefer Melody." He winks and I can feel my cheeks flush ever so slightly.

SEVEN

MELODY

The afternoon passes in a heartbeat. After we had something to eat, we played with the kids and I don't think I've ever laughed so much in my life. My face actually hurts right now. We sit down on a bench, just to recharge for a minute before leaving. It takes Ozzy all of thirty seconds to fall asleep in Logan's arms.

"Do you want me to carry your picnic basket to the car whilst you carry Ozzy?" Logan takes a deep breath before he responds, "No, it's okay thanks. We walked here. Just hand me the basket after I've adjusted him." I can't let him carry him all the way back home.

"Logan, come and get in my car. I'll drop you both home. I've already got two booster seats in the back anyway as I normally drive Ozzy around." Logan nods appreciatively and follows me and Zach to my car. We get the boys in without a problem and start the five-minute drive to his house. That's when it hits me. He told me the other day and I haven't once asked what is going on.

"Logan, why did Gabriella have a hospital appointment?" He looks up from his phone with an apprehensive look in his eyes.

"I'm sure she'll tell you all about it next time she sees you." The tension in the air is thick and it's clear this is something he doesn't want to discuss with me now. So I leave it, pushing him won't do any good for anyone.

We pull up outside the house and Ozzy wakes up just as Logan unbuckles his belt.

"Daddy, can Zach come in? just for a minute"

He looks over to me at the same time as Zach and I don't want to say no but the thought of seeing Gabriella right now makes me a little uneasy.

"Okay, but only for a few minutes though as you need to get to bed." Both boys leap around excitedly and jump out of the car, running towards the front door.

"Come on doll, I'll make you a coffee. Gabby isn't here right now but I know she'll be sad to have missed you." I want to ask questions about where she is but it's not my place. Getting out of the car, I follow Logan as he lets himself in. The boys run straight into Ozzy's bedroom as we make our way to the kitchen. It feels strange being here without Gabriella but somehow, he fits right in. I take a seat on one of the tall chairs and watch Logan get to work.

"Thanks for today, Melody. I'm sorry again for the misunderstanding the other day. I'm not always so paranoid. It's just this whole situation is so crazy, it's hard to get my head around. And seeing you after what happened, it threw me. What are the fucking chances?" What are the chances that my one-time crazy hook-up would turn out to be my friend's husband? The whole time Logan is talking, he has his back to me, making us a drink.

"It's okay, Logan. I'm just glad we cleared up that I'm not a crazy stalker." Logan turns to me with a smile on his face.

"There's my funny girl." I placed my drink down, and his

eyes meet mine as he pushes himself in between my legs, placing his hands either side of me on the counter behind, boxing me in.

"D'you know something, doll? You are so beautiful when you smile." His smell invades my nostrils and I feel my heart speed up as he moves his hand towards my face, stroking a stray hair behind my ear. Something so trivial and meaningless to most, has me feeling all sorts of things right now. Placing his index finger under my chin, he lifts my head. Our eyes meet as he slowly lowers his mouth to mine.

"Logan, stop." This is wrong. He hesitates for a moment,

"What if I don't want to stop, Melody?" speaking with his lips brushing against mine.

The cocksure look in his eyes is all it takes to break the trance he has me in.

"You're married Logan. And what makes it worse is the fact your wife is a good friend of mine. You may be used to this whole using people for sex thing, but that isn't me."

Feeling my anger rise, I push him away as I stand and head towards Ozzy's room.

Fuck.

When I open the bedroom door, I see the boys curled up on the bed. Fast asleep. I hear him before I know he is behind me,

"It's okay, just leave him here tonight. Give me a call when you're up in the morning and I'll come and drop him off. Or you pick him up, whatever is easiest for you." I'd love nothing more than to tell him to fuck off, but the boys are used to being left to sleep. Wherever they are, we normally leave them be and just drop them off the next day. I don't want to risk upsetting either of them, so I know it's best that Zach stays.

"Okay, I'll leave him. But I'm only doing this for them. I want you to stay the hell away from me. I feel bad enough for what I've done. I could never be with you again, knowing what I know now. I hope you sleep well tonight Logan because I can honestly say that I won't. Don't see me out, I already know the way. I'll message you when I'm awake." I turn and walk away before Logan has the chance to reply.

It's less than a ten-minute drive home but I think I manage to cry for most of it. I'm crying because I'm angry at myself. I was so wrapped up in everything that is Logan Pierce that I let myself trust him. I can't believe I had sex with Gabriella's husband.

The guilt that I buried hits hard. Knowing it's for the best, I pull over and send Avery a text. I'm not sure I can risk telling her face to face that her son is staying with Zach's Dad. She replies right away, letting me know that she is gonna have a long soak in the bath. At least that gives me the chance to calm down a bit before I get back to the house.

After a five-minute pep talk, I make my way home. Checking myself in the mirror before I get out of the car, in case Avery isn't in the bath yet. I'm looking about as good as I can considering.

All is quiet in the living room as I enter, so that's a good sign. I try to sneak into my bedroom as Avery calls out from the bathroom

"Dee, was everything okay today? What's the plan tomorrow with Zack?" I clear my throat before I dare answer

"Everything was good. I said I'll message when I wake up and I'll go and get him so you can have a lie in or go shopping. Just do whatever you want, okay? I got this." Hopefully, she doesn't pick up that anything is wrong by the wobble in my voice.

"Okay, Dee, thank you. I don't know where I'd be without you. I love you."

"Love you too, Ree. Anything for you guys. I'm just gonna head to bed now as I feel wiped out after today." To be fair, that wasn't a lie. I do feel exhausted. Physically and emotionally.

"Okay, night Dee". I can't bring myself to speak anymore through fear of breaking down. I hate lying to my best friend. Well, I'm not technically lying, I'm just not telling her the whole truth. I omitted that the boys aren't with Gabriella, but in my defense, it's not my fault she didn't ask. Going into my room, I get myself ready for bed. Wiping away the tears turns out to be a pointless exercise as they keep on coming. I feel awful about what I have done. Knowing that I can't handle seeing Avery anytime soon, I go online and book her a room at her favorite hotel. We have the money so I can spin it as a treat from me. It'll give me some much-needed time to think about everything that has gone on. She responds immediately, so I go and pack her bag whilst she finishes in the bath. I leave her a little note, reminding her I've gone to bed in the hope that she doesn't come into my room and see me like this. My phone lights up on my bedside table and I see it's Avery, thanking me. What she doesn't know is that I need this just as much as she does. Time to clear my head and spend some time with Zach is the best thing now.

I just hope that I can face Gabriella soon and find out what the Hell is going on.

Sleep came a lot easier than expected. Turns out that the guilty do sleep well after all. It's still early when I wake so I decide to try and cleanse myself in the shower before having to face Logan again. I draw everything out as long as possible and I'm guessing as he hasn't text me, that everything is okay with the boys. After slowly eating breakfast, I know that I can't draw this out any longer. So, I grab my phone and text Logan to let him know that I'm coming to get Zack. When I pick up my phone, I see I already have a text from Logan, informing me that he will be here with the kids, very soon.

Twenty minutes pass and they still haven't arrived yet, so I call him. I know it's only twenty minutes, but he lives five minutes away and it's freaking me out. He answers on the first ring

"Hey, sorry, doll. The kids wanted ice cream and I didn't wanna say no. I'll be with you in five. Would you like any ice cream?"

"Logan, it's 10am, I think I'll give it a miss." Who has ice cream at 10am? Oh, that's right, kids.

"Okay, doll, but you don't know what you're missing." With that, he hangs up.

True to his word, he arrives five minutes later. Zack and Ozzy come bursting through the door, followed by Logan. I barely have time to get up before Logan is in my living room, eating ice cream like a four-year-old.

"Looks like you're enjoying that, Logan." I smile for the sake of the kids, "Maybe you'd enjoy it more in the car?" He breezes past me, making his way further in,

"It's almost the best thing I've ever tasted" as he winks at me, ignoring my subtle attempt to get him to leave. I can feel my cheeks start to burn, knowing exactly what he is insinuating. So, I try my best to pretend that it didn't happen and make my way into the kitchen, whilst listening to Logan chuckle. I'm still mad at him about yesterday and it would do me good to not forget that. Knowing that Zach and Ozzy are playing happily in Zach's room, I automatically do the thing I would do for anyone.

"Would you like a drink, Mr. Pierce?" The words leave a slightly bitter taste on my tongue. I'm supposed to be avoiding this man and yet I have just given him reason to stay. It must be his testosterone that makes my brain not function as it should. What is this man doing to me? The look on his face is almost comical.

"Mr. Pierce? I think I like the sound of that coming from your mouth." Again, I can feel my face burning but I only have myself to blame this time.

He can sense my discomfort as he makes his way towards me, licking those damn lips of his. So, I busy myself to pull my attention away from him.

"You have got to try this, Melody. It is as close to heaven as I'm likely to get."

With a look of the devil in his eyes, he takes a scoop out of his cup as I shake my head and attempt to turn away from him once more. He comes at me from the side and spins me around, pinning me in place against the counter with his body. Moving the spoonful of ice cream towards me. I close my mouth and shake my head vigorously, refusing him entry. He doesn't stop his hand from coming at me and I end up with ice cream all over my chin and cheeks. As I open my mouth to tell him to stop, he shoves the spoon in with what little ice cream it has left on it.

Closing my lips around the spoon, he slowly pulls it out.

"See Melody, heaven. It looks like you missed a bit though." Before I wipe it away, he licks the side of my face.

"Eww Logan, that's disgusting." My mouth utters the words, but my body seems to disagree as butterflies dance in the most inappropriate of places. He lets go of me and steps back, all the while laughing his head off. His laughter seems to be contagious as I find myself laughing along with him. In all honesty, if that had been anyone else, I would've probably slapped them. I pick up the tea towel and clean off the rest of my face whilst he polishes off his ice cream. Zack then comes bursting into the kitchen.

"Dee dee, will Mommy be home soon or is it a Dee and Zee day?" I've always called our days the Dee and Zee days. There was a time when he had a bit of separation anxiety from his Mom, so I tried to make it a fun thing. Luckily, it worked a treat.

"it's a Dee and Zee day today, little dude." Zack is obviously happy with that answer as he goes running out of the kitchen singing.

"Dee and Zee are gonna save the world today". I can't help but smile at the little dude. No man has ever made me as happy as that kid. As I look up, I notice Logan watching me, and I feel the need to tell him why.

"Avery has gone away. Well, I've sent her away. She's gone for two nights, last night being the first. She never gets a break and as I had the time off, I decided that it was time for her to treat herself. So, I packed her bags, booked her a room and sent her on her way. The money that we earned from your music video put us in a decent financial position, so I told her to make the most of it, as I am never doing that again for her." Logan almost looks hurt by that remark, but he just shrugs his shoulders and heads out of the kitchen. I hear him calling Ozzy and when I walk into the living room, he is helping Ozzy put his shoes on.

"Are you going already?" I feel pathetic as the words tumble out of my mouth.

"Yeah. I have a few things that need to be taken care of at the record label and Ozzy is staying with his grandparents tonight. I've already packed his stuff so I'm gonna drop him with them as soon as I'm done." I flash him a smile and then busy myself clearing the table. I almost don't want to admit this, but I've had fun with Logan. Every time we are together, all we seem to do is laugh. I've never felt this at ease with a man before. I have to keep reminding myself that this one is off-limits. What happened in the past, has to stay there. I didn't know he was married when we did what we did. That's all on him. But it still doesn't change how I feel when I'm near him and his ability to give me temporary amnesia.

"Okay then, have a nice time Ozzy and I'll see you soon. Sleepover soon?" Ozzy nods like a possessed child. As they head towards the door, Logan turns and goes to say something but then he shakes his head. He opens the door and Ozzy goes dashing towards the car. Logan unlocks it from the doorstep and Ozzy jumps in.

"Bye Logan." He turns and looks at me

"Bye doll." He almost looks sad as he walks away. I don't let myself read too much into that, being sure to close the door before he has a chance to look back. Every time he looks at me with those big blue eyes, I feel as if he can see the real me. I feel as though he can read my mind. Therefore, he knows how I'm feeling each time we are together. I don't have too much time to think about it all though, as I can hear Zack calling me. I know right here, right now, that this is the last time that I will get a moment alone today.

EIGHT

LOGAN

L eaving Melody then was hard. Everything inside wanted me to stay.

It's been a crazy few days. I'm so angry with myself for not listening to Oz when he was desperately trying to tell me who she was. It took just under twenty-four hours for me to calm down enough to finally listen to him. He was so mad at me for shouting at 'his Dee dee', it was cute. If it wasn't for him pestering me then I'm not sure I would have ever bothered reaching out to her. The guilt was horrible and I'm not normally the type of person who apologizes, even when I know I'm wrong. Meeting her at the park was the best thing though. She accepted my apology with grace. And the right amount of sarcasm, I loved it. Making a pass at her wasn't one of my finest moments, especially in Gabby's house. I couldn't help myself though, she does something to me that I've never felt before. Her rejection hit me like a slap in the face.

She didn't need to remind me that I'm married, that is

something I would never forget but it's also something that she could never understand.

I don't need to be told that I should stay away from her, I already know it, but that doesn't stop me. Thank the lord that Zach fell asleep with Oz because that gave me the perfect reason to see her again. And boy, what a treat that was. I couldn't resist touching her. Any kind of contact eases my crazy mind and gives me peace, even for just a minute. I had to walk away when I licked her face, to hide what was going on in my pants.

The drive to the record label office is longer than I'd like but I'm enjoying the time with my little man. I didn't really want him to stay with his grandparents yet, but he was missing them, so I knew it was the best thing to do. This is the life he is used to, so I don't want to mess with it for now. His night with Zach seems to have wiped him out as by the time we arrive, he is fast asleep.

"Come on Oz, time to get out of the car." Picking him up out of his seat, it hits him where we are,

"We go and see Belle?" He's talking about Belinda, one of the owners PA's. The first time he met her, she was wearing a yellow dress and he misheard when I said her name.

"Yes Oz, we go and see Belle."

Oz had watched Beauty and the Beast that day and immediately named her Belle. I thought he would forget about it, but Cody made sure he didn't. We can all see that Belinda finds it a bit uncomfortable when Cody calls her that, but she's shy and timid so she never says a word. Ozzy fights to get out of my arms as we reach the office, running straight to Belinda.

"Belle!" He screams, running towards her with a huge smile on his face. She crouches down and scoops him up as soon as he reaches her.

"Prince Ozzy, what may I do for you on this fine day sir." His face warms my heart.

"You so silly, Belle." They both laugh as we enter the meeting room. Belinda places Oz in the chair at the head of the table, placing her notepad and pens down for him.

Most of the band are here already with the exception of Cody, who arrives as soon as I have finished greeting everyone.

"Holy shit Logan, I didn't realize that my main man would be here today. Hey Oz, what's hanging dude?" Ozzy laughs as Cody reaches out his fist for him, which he bumps immediately. His face soon changes when he sees the ice cream in Cody's hand. Cody notices his face change and turns to me.

"Is it okay if I take him to get an ice cream, L?" We haven't even signed any paperwork yet and he is already looking for an excuse to leave.

"He's already had some ice cream, man. Maybe next time?"

"But Daddy…" Ozzy's face breaks.

"Yeah… But Daddy. Come on, man, I don't get to see the kid often. Let me treat him. It doesn't have to be ice cream." These two sad faces are gonna be the death of me.

"Okay, but don't let him eat too much as he is going to his grandparents straight after. Also, no using my kids to pick up women." Shock resonates on Cody's face as he pretends to be offended.

"I'm a fucking rock God, Logan, I do not need a kid to pick up women. Anyway, I only did that once I don't see why you feel the need to keep using that against me." Ozzy erupts in laughter behind him, and I shoot Cody a look. My kid is smart, he knows the difference between good and bad words but that doesn't stop him from laughing when he hears Cody swear. Ozzy jumps off the chair and runs to Cody, grabbing his hand before I change my mind.

"Oz, I'm trusting you to look after Uncle Cody, okay?" Vigorous nodding the head followed by a cross sign made over his heart, "And don't let him talk to any strange women."

SHARON CORREIA

Looking up to Cody, he too crosses his heart. Before they make it out the door, Cody stops and looks over to Belinda,

"Would you like something to suck on Belle's? Coz I'm always happy to help you out with that one." Belinda's face goes beet red as she tries her hardest to ignore him, shuffling around the paperwork in front of her. Hunter pipes up as soon as he looks at her,

"Jesus Christ, Code, leave the poor girl alone." A few seconds of awkwardness passes as Hunter pipes up again, "I'll come with you to get ice cream, I fancy something sweet. I can also keep an eye on Oz then." Cody's shoulders sag in defeat as Hunter follows him out the door. Me and Eddie exchange a look as Spencer shoots up, running after them,

"Wait for me guys."

Eddie looks a mixture of relieved and pissed off as he looks over to Belinda,

"Can I just get this shit done please, Belinda? I can think of a million other things I'd rather be doing right now." Eddie has been clean for a while now. Although I'm not worried he's using again, he does seem to be distracted lately.

"Everything okay, man?" He nods, sheepishly with a shrug.

"Nothing to be concerned about. Just family shit. Having the surname Worthington comes with its own set of bullshit that I can't seem to get away from." I know he doesn't want to talk about it, so I leave it for now. He'll talk when he's ready. Belinda waits patiently for us to finish. She needs to get a bit more forceful if she wants to make it in this industry. Rock stars are notoriously self-involved, and they have a habit of thinking the world revolves around them. She only has us to look after so far, as her boss thought we were the best band to introduce her to the industry. He's probably right as we have got most things out of our system. Eddie moved away from the party life as soon as he got clean, knowing it was all or nothing for him. I never really partied much at any stage, my life wasn't meant to be that way.

50

Cody, Hunter and Spencer though, that's a different story. They don't bring anything on the tour bus, in front of me and Eddie but we know they live their lives to the fullest, enjoying everything this life has to offer. I envy them at times, but I know it isn't for me. I just want to make music. If I get to go out on tour, seeing the fans then that's a huge bonus. Live music is where my heart lies, and I will do everything in my power to make sure I always get to do it.

The guys arrive back just as I finish up the paperwork I needed to do. Seeing the smile on Ozzy's face lets me know I made the right decision, letting him go.

"Hey boy, did you have a good time with your uncles?" He nods as he climbs on my lap, smelling sweet. "And did you look after your Uncle Cody? He didn't try and pick up any strays, did he?" Cody pipes up before Ozzy answers.

"I will have you know that I only have eyes for one girl. My Belle is where it's at for me. I'm just waiting for her to finally realize that I am everything she wants in a man." He looks over to Belinda as she hands off Hunter's paperwork to him. She doesn't reply, as usual. Instead, she pushes Cody's paperwork towards him and eyeballs him, waiting for him to sign it. "Why you gotta treat me like this in front of my boys, Princess. You know you love me, just admit it." Belinda doesn't admit anything. Instead, she goes a nice shade of red as she finally opens her mouth to reply. We are all on the edge of our seat, waiting to see if she breaks.

"Could you please sign that Cody as I have to get it copied and filed as soon as possible." All our shoulders sag in disappointment. But Cody does as she ask's, immediately. Standing up, with Ozzy in my arms, I know it's time to leave. His Grandparents will no doubt be calling me any moment to find out where we are.

"I'm out guys." We all say our goodbyes as I leave. Strapping Ozzy back into the car I am reminded of Melody. I'm annoyed with myself as this is something I have done endless times before, but now I link it with her. How Ozzy smells right now doesn't help that either. Smelling the sweet ice cream smell coming off my boy makes me think of licking her face. She's the best thing I've ever tasted. I'm gonna do everything I can to make sure that I get to taste her again.

NINE

MELODY

I wasn't wrong, Zach didn't let me have a moment's rest all day. On the plus side, Dee and Zee day was a huge success according to Zach. By 8.30pm, I finally manage to sit down with the glass of wine that I've been craving for the last couple of hours. I love that boy as if he were my own, but lord does he tire me out. There's nothing on TV that I want to watch so I take the time to turn on the laptop and sort my emails. Before the laptop has fully fired up, I've already finished my first glass of wine. So, I go into the kitchen and bring the bottle with me, saving time in the long run. I have a quick scan through social media, Avery has posted loads of pictures. I'm so glad that she's enjoying herself. People assume, because she is a model/actress that she leads a glamorous lifestyle but that couldn't be further from the truth. It seems that half the year is spent scrimping and saving whilst the other half is comfortable. Fortunately, we are in the comfortable stage right now, thanks to Guilty Pleasure and their music video. Speaking of Guilty Pleasure, I know I haven't seen any of their music videos before. I'm pretty sure Avery has played their music, but I've never really paid attention. She usually has her music blasting whilst she cleans so I tend to take myself off to my room or leave the house completely. So, I need to know right now, what all the fuss is about. Typing the words Guilty Pleasure into my search engine, I click on the first music video I see. I haven't got a clue what I am letting myself in for so there is no point in worrying about how old it is.

Twenty minutes and four videos later, I can now see what all the fuss is about. These boys are amazing. Not to mention, smoking hot. I never got to meet the other band members when I was on set, as they weren't around. I can honestly say that not a single one of them was touched with the ugly stick. The bassist has got the most beautiful brown eyes I think I have ever seen. I'm pretty sure that they must enhance the darkness of his eyes when they edit the video, because that can't be natural. They all fall short when compared to Mr. Logan Pierce though. He is hands down, the best-looking guy in the band. Watching these videos and the way that Logan looks into the camera takes me back to the first time I looked into his eyes. This man commands his audience, his eyes demand your full attention. I click on to the next video and just as it starts to play, there is a knock at the door. I put the laptop down and as I stand, I feel the effects of the —now two—glasses of wine. I stumble to the door and open it without checking who it is.

"Hey Melody, are you okay?" I nod and look up. That's when I see the same eyes that I have been looking into for the past twenty minutes or so.

"Oh shit, hey Logan. Umm, yeah, I'm fine. Just got up too fast, that's all. Everything okay? Why are you here?" That smile will be my undoing, I'm sure.

"I forgot to give you Zach's coat earlier. I just found it in the car and thought that you might need it." Taking the coat from him, my hand brushes his. It feels like an electric shock travels up my arm, leaving me with a tingling in my most intimate area.

"Thanks."

Biting my lip, I try to scramble my thoughts together. Nothing seems to make sense when he is near.

"Oz is with his Grandparents and I was just driving by, so it made sense to drop it with you." The look on his face is cute and his awkwardness doesn't go unnoticed,

"Can I hear… It is, isn't it…" Logan pushes past me and makes his way into the living room. At first, I stand in the doorway, confused. That is until I realize what he heard. The embarrassment I feel now has me wanting to be swallowed up by a big, black hole. Slowly, I make my way into the living room. I see him, sitting in my seat looking at the laptop with a huge, shit eating grin. I can feel the flush on my face but honestly, I'm not sure if that is the situation that I'm in, or the wine.

Stepping across, I grab the nearly empty bottle and walk over to my glass. Standing between Logan and the laptop being sure to shut it down as I refill.

"If it wasn't for the fact that you just made my view better, I may have been offended by that. What's up, doll? Needed your Mr. Pierce fix, did ya? Didn't get enough of the real thing earlier? I'm always just a phone call away if you ever need to scratch that itch again." I interrupt him before he continues because I have a feeling he may go on for a while.

"Actually, it was research. You are going to be releasing a video soon that I am starring in. So, I wanted to make sure that you looked half decent on screen." I take a seat on the chair next to him. The other seat is filled with the days laundry that I was planning on folding later. I can feel him looking at me as I place my feet up on the chair and take a sip of my wine.

"C'mon funny girl, I'm just messing with you." I can see that the sincerity in his face is real, "I'm honored that you've taken the time to check out the band. So, tell me, what did you think?" My mind is full of different insults to throw in his direction. But, because I'm full of the Dutch courage I go with honesty.

"I loved it. I didn't think that I would like your music because it's not what I normally listen to. But it's safe to say that I've really enjoyed it so far." Logan is currently grinning like the cat that got the cream so it's time to knock him down a peg or two.

"And all the other guys are hot as well. I mean, a girl is spoilt for choice with your band." Smiling smugly as I take another sip of wine. Logan shakes off the disappointment and puffs out his chest.

"Not a patch on the lead singer though, hey, doll." I roll my eyes and laugh, as if I'm disagreeing with him. But in reality, he couldn't be more right.

We spend the next few hours talking about nothing in particular. The time passed so fast, I didn't realize it was getting so late until I feel my eyes starting to droop.

"Hey, I better go before you fall asleep. You've insulted me enough tonight. I don't want to be accused of making you fall asleep on me as well. I don't think my ego could take it." His words hit me like a cold bucket of water, I'm now wide eyed and ready to go. But as I get to my feet to follow Logan to the door, my head starts pounding. Normally, I don't drink on my own, but I felt like I needed it tonight. He opens the door and takes a step outside.

"So, I guess I'll see you soon, sleepy." Just another pet name to add to the list.

"Yeah, I guess so, Mr. Pierce." The look on his face and the glint in his eyes has me feeling all sorts of things. I know this thing between us isn't going to go anywhere but I can't ignore the sparks that fly between us when we are together.

TEN

LOGAN

Every time she calls me Mr. Pierce, I get a vision of her bent over in front of me, her hair wrapped around one hand pulling her head back, with my handprint on her ass. This, of course, makes me instantly hard. I've had an amazing time with her tonight. In fact, it's the best time I've ever spent with a woman that didn't involve getting naked. This is something different with us. I feel like we could be friends even though I am insanely attracted to her.

"How about we take the boys to the park again tomorrow? Say 10:30ish?" She nods as her cheeks flush. I like Melody when she's had a drink.

I don't want to ruin it by overstepping the mark, but I also can't walk away without taking a chance. Before she reacts, I grab her upper arms as I crash my lips to hers. I expect her to push me away but instead, she leans into me, so I wrap my arms around her and go for the kill. Opening my mouth, I slide my tongue in, and to my surprise, I am greeted by the warmth of hers as it thrashes against mine. She starts to move her arms up my stomach, towards my chest. As her hands reach my face, I pull away.

"Thanks for tonight, doll. It's been a blast." It would be so easy to take advantage of her right now. The look on her face is enough to tell me I had her where I wanted her. But instead, I turn and walk away. It takes everything within me to do this, but I know it's the right thing. I can't risk looking at her again until I am locked away in my car and the look on her face nearly breaks me. Turning on the engine, I drive away before I change my mind.

That expression will forever be etched in my brain. A mixture of confusion and disappointment haunts me as I make the short drive home. As I pull up to the house, I see that all the lights are off, letting me know that Gabby has gone to bed. This is confirmed as I let myself in when I am greeted by nothing but darkness. Not wanting to disturb Gabby, I go straight to my bedroom and shut myself in the bathroom. I should probably check on her but I'm sure if there was a problem, she would've called me. Stripping off, I turn on the shower, making sure the water is cold. I don't know if this works but it's worth a shot. The cold hits me hard and seems to have the desired effect after a while. Once I'm satisfied, but not in the way I'd like, I get out of the shower and head into my room. Even though I paid for it, this has always been Gabby's home. But it still feels odd, being in what was once the guest room. Still, I'm here for my boy if he ever needs anything so I wouldn't have it any other way. People have no idea what is going on with Gabby right now and honestly, it's not my story to tell. One day, everyone will know, and things will change. I wish Gabby would let people in, but she has to do things her way and I am in no position to argue with her.

Getting under the sheets, it feels good to lie down. Checking my phone one last time, secretly hoping that Melody messaged me, begging me to come back. But nothing. I fire off a quick message to Ozzy's grandparents, letting them know that I need him dropped off an hour earlier as he has a playdate. It's late, so I don't expect a reply, but I get one anyway. Turns out Ozzy has only just gone to sleep. Probably because of all the sugar in his system. Laughing to myself, I don't reply. I'll apologize in the morning when I see them. As I get comfortable, my mind wanders back to Melody. The look on her face when she snorts after laughing uncontrollably. The flush in her cheeks if things get too intense. The way she bites her lip when she gets nervous. How have I never noticed this on anyone else before? The simple movements from her would have me on my knees in a heartbeat if she would let me. But the best, and equally worst look was tonight, as I left. Knowing that she wanted more, she has never looked so beautiful. If I'm honest, I braced myself for a slap in the face as I made my move but what I got back was worse. I could feel the need in her kiss as it matched my own but feeling her hands on me had me hard as a rock in an instant. Melody Grace is the last thing on my mind as I slowly drift off to sleep, and I know that even in slumber, her beautiful face won't leave me.

I wake early and have another cold shower. Only this time, it didn't work. So, after spending longer in the shower than I planned, I'm just about ready as Gabby's parents arrive.

"Hey Little man, did you have a good time with Mee-maw and Paw-paw?" Ozzy runs into my open arms and I lift him up.

"Yes Daddy. I had the best time. We seeing Zach today?" I nod, confirming his excitement. He wiggles out of my arms and runs to his room, leaving me with Jenny and Des.

"How are things, Logan?" I know what they're insinuating but I'm not getting into this now.

"It's as well as can be expected, given the circumstances."
Before they can probe any further, Ozzy comes dashing back in.
"Ready Daddy." Normally I'd tell him off for being rude, but
he's saved me, so I'll let this one go.

"Ready little man. I'm guessing you're sticking around to
spend some time with Gabby?" Jenny and Des both nod. "She's
still asleep right now so make yourselves comfortable." They
make their way past me, towards the kitchen as we make our
way out the door. Ozzy's excitement radiates off him on the
journey to the park. I'd like to think it's his excitement I'm
feeling but I know it's my own.

I see Melody in the distance as we pull up in the park, but I
don't let Ozzy know she's here yet. I want a moment to watch
her, without anyone knowing. It feels kinda wrong, watching
someone whilst they carry on, blissfully unaware but it gives me
a guilty thrill, seeing how she acts when I'm not there. She
smiles over to Zach and right now, I'd pay good money for her to
look at me the same way. I don't deserve it. She also doesn't
deserve to get dragged into the fucked-up situation I'm in. I have
no right feeling like this, Melody isn't mine to fawn over, but I
want to soak in these moments whilst it's still possible. Life is
short and I want to live it to the fullest.

ELEVEN

MELODY

I arrived at the park just before 10.30 and set up all the toys and games I brought for the kids. Truth be told, I wanted as much distraction as possible. This is the first time that I've seen Logan since he left me speechless on my doorstep and that can't happen again. I'm mad at him for leaving me like that but I'm madder at myself for letting him kiss me in the first place. Zach indicates the arrival of Ozzy and Logan by letting out his usual high-pitched squeal before jumping up and taking off in their direction. I look up and see Logan making his way towards me as the kids head off towards the climbers. I busy myself again by re-organizing the toys, anything to stop myself from staring at this beautiful man.

"Hey doll, you okay? I didn't bring a picnic as I thought I'd treat you and the kids to a burger or something. That sound okay with you?" Looking up, I nod.

"No burger for me though. I've got work later and I won't fit into my uniform if I eat too much." I laugh to myself knowing this is true. I know I'm not fat and I have no concerns in that area, but my uniform can be very unforgiving and the last thing I need is a burger belly. Looking up, I see Logan staring at me with a look of anger in his eyes.

"Just how tight is this uniform of yours that you can't even have a decent sized dinner?" His rage subsides slightly as he awaits my answer. Not wanting any questions, I make it brief,

"My uniform is fine. I just prefer to have something small so that I am not uncomfortable during my shift." I'm not ashamed of my job, I just don't want to talk about it now, when we are with the boys. He sits down on the blanket and gives me a "Hmmm".

Before he has time to think about it, I start talking about the kids and how much fun they always have when they are together. This seems to do the trick as he is looking over at the kids with a smile. He turns to look at me and opens his mouth as if he's about to say something. But before the words come out, the kids come running over,

"Daddy, can we get some food please? I'm hungry." Logan brings Ozzy in for a hug and replies,

"Well, I suppose you did have breakfast at 6am so it makes perfect sense that you are hungry already. Come on then, let's help pack up."

We make short work of packing everything away and I run it over to the car whilst Logan starts walking the boys over to the little diner nearby. I catch up with them just as they are sitting down.

"Dee dee, you can sit next to Ozzy's Daddy. We want to sit next to each other, okay?" I can't really start an argument with a seven-year-old in the middle of a diner, can I? I smile shyly at Logan as I take a seat next to him. Risking a glance at him, I can't help but roll my eyes at the smug grin on his face.

"It's okay, doll, I don't bite." He winks, "Well, not unless you ask nicely." At that moment I have a flashback to the trailer. The memory of his teeth on my skin gives me goosebumps and I visibly shudder. Hearing Logan chuckle next to me brings me crashing back to the here and now, so I turn towards him and give him a playful slap on the arm. Before he can respond, the waitress interrupts.

"Can I take your orders please?" All the boys order themselves a burger, but I decide to stick to a salad. Logan huffs at me as I order but I ignore him. I refuse to have any confrontation in front of the kids. Before too long, the waitress comes back out with our food. Logan shakes his head as she puts down my salad. As soon as we get the boys plates ready, we all start eating.

"Wow, Mr. Pierce. You seem to be really enjoying that burger. The noises coming from your throat are disturbing. Are you always like that when you eat?" With a sinister look in his eyes, he responds,

"Only when things taste good, doll." He winks at me before continuing. "Do you wanna bite? It's so good." I know what he is trying to do and it's not going to work.

"No thank you, I am enjoying my salad." He shrugs as he continues,

"Suit yourself but you really don't know what you're missing." Oh no. I want a burger now, I have a serious case of food envy. He must notice the moment I regret my salad choice as he keeps wafting his burger in my direction. I try my best to ignore him but the more he does it, the more I want that damn burger. The sound coming from him now is pure evil. He leans into me slightly and starts waving his burger under my nose. The teasing is too much now so I strike. Before he pulls away, I grab his wrist and take a huge bite.

"Hey, that's my burger." I can feel the sauce dripping down my chin, but I don't care.

"I regret nothing, that was soo good. You were right, it is amazing." Puppy dog-like eyes stare back at me as I grab a napkin off the table and clean up the mess I've made of my face.

We all finish off our own food and we send the kids over to look at the dessert cart. The waitress comes over as the boys leave and stops next to Logan.

"I didn't wanna do this in front of the kids, but can I have your autograph please? And maybe a photo?" It takes me a minute to catch on. I know how I met Logan, but I forgot that he's in a band. A smile takes over his face as he stands and addresses the waitress.

"Of course..." He looks down at her badge before continuing, "Sally. It would be my pleasure." She gets out her phone and takes at least half a dozen photos of the two of them, making sure to get the best angles. They laugh and joke as they go through the photos, talking about which one should be her next profile picture. He politely asks her not to say where they are but to make sure to put it on the fan page, letting everyone know what a great tipper he is. He winks at her and her whole face goes red, hugging her phone to her chest. I see that it isn't just me he has that effect on it seems. He signs the napkin in front of him but just before she walks away, she turns and looks at us both.

"Can I just say, you two make a beautiful couple. Love looks good on you both." As I go to correct her, Logan places his arm around my shoulder.

"Aww, thanks, Sally. She's definitely a keeper." She scurries off with a noticeable skip in her step.

"Jesus Logan, you can't say shit like that." Before he replies, the boys come running back, cake in hand. Logan whips his arm away before they sit down but I don't think they would've noticed if he hadn't. They're too busy stuffing their faces full of cake. The guilt is etched on Logan's face as he looks at Ozzy. It's another reminder of how I have no right to feel the way I do every time Logan is near. The trouble is every time he is near me everything else fades away and all I see is him. The other thing that I hadn't thought about until a couple of minutes ago, is the fact that he's famous. He is likely to get recognized everywhere he goes. How would it look if someone took a photo when he had his arm around me? This whole situation is so messed up.

"Dee dee, I'm talking to you. Can we go to the climbers again?" Shaking my head back to reality, I look at my watch and see the time.

"Shit. I'm gonna be late for work. We've gotta go." Zach instantly looks sad. I knew this was going to happen, but I planned on giving him warning until I got lost in my head.

"But Dee dee, I don't wanna go yet." The sadness in his expression just about breaks my heart.

"I know dude, but we really have to. Mommy really wants to spend some time with you." With the simple mention of his Mom, he sheepishly nods and gets down from his chair. I jump in and give Ozzy a big squeeze, feeling Logan's eyes on me as I do.

"Thanks for today. Next time lunch is on me." Logan smiles as I make my way to the door.

"So, there will be a next time then." I walk away, not giving him the answer he is looking for. Everything in me knows there shouldn't be a next time. I just hope my heart and my head can agree.

TWELVE

LOGAN

I thought I went too far then. Thought I'd ruined the chance to see Melody again. Even though she didn't answer me back, her body told me that there would be a next time. When she shuts out the world around her, I know I have her, but as soon as she is reminded of my situation, she backs off. I can't wait for the day I can finally let her in. But even then, she may still run. I don't know if she can handle the truth of Gabby's situation, but something has to give, and soon.

Ozzy decided that he didn't wanna go back to the park if Zach wasn't with him, so we make the short drive home. Jenny and Des' car has gone when I get back, which takes me by surprise as I thought they were having Oz again tonight. He doesn't seem to notice so we make our way inside. Jenny is sitting in the living room and Ozzy goes and jumps on her lap.

"Mee-maw! Where's Paw-paw?" She looks lovingly at the boy as he wiggles away on her.

"Paw-paw has popped out quickly. Go and pack your bag and

he should be back by the time you're done." Ozzy jumps off her lap and runs into his bedroom.

"Hey Jenny, everything okay?" She gets to her feet and guides me into the kitchen.

"Des has taken Gabriella home. I don't want to argue over this Logan, but she needs someone with her 24/7 and you simply can't do that. She still doesn't want to admit that anything is wrong. I'm scared of her being on her own and what she might do to herself." I have nothing left in me to argue.

"What about Ozzy?"

"Ozzy can stay with us whenever you need him to. He is the only thing keeping her going right now. The drugs have messed her up, Logan. I need her to be with us so I can watch her. It isn't what she wants but we didn't give her a choice." Ozzy comes crashing into the kitchen before I can take this conversation any further. But I know this is for the best. I can't give Gabby the time she needs. At least with Jenny and Des I know they can keep a close eye on her whilst Ozzy is being taken care of too. I've been trying to keep myself so busy that I failed to see how bad things had got. We make our way into the living room just as Des comes through the front door. He shoots me a nod as Ozzy runs into his open arms.

"Paw-paw, where have you been?" Releasing Oz, he takes his bag off him as he crouches down to his eye level.

"I was just taking Mommy to our house and getting her settled. She wanted a sleepover with us. isn't that great?" Ozzy wraps his arms around his neck and lets him know how excited he is. Standing to his feet, taking Ozzy with him, Des turns to address me.

"This isn't personal son, and you're welcome to get the boy whenever you want him, okay?"

"I know pops, we're all just doing what's best. Please don't hesitate to call me if you need anything. Anything at all. Family first." Des always told me family first the moment I first met him. He may be Gabby's Dad, but I've always had a close relationship with him. He insisted I call him pops the day we told them Gabby was pregnant. So much has happened in that time, it seems like a lifetime ago.

We say our goodbyes and the moment they pull away, my mind drifts to Melody. She is innocent in this whole messed up situation and I know I should walk away. So why do I want to call her so bad? Hearing her voice is what I need but deep down, I know that isn't enough. It will never be enough for me so that's why I know I have to keep my distance. Thankfully, I have some shit to do with the music video because the record label called and told me they want to release it sooner than originally planned. The video is ready to go, and they want to drop it as soon as we all sign off on it. That comes with its own problems, I know I have to look at Melody's face once again as she gets off on camera. But this really does seem like the lesser of two evils. I know if I stay here on my own, I will give in and call her. Fuck, I'd even hunt her down if I had to and find out where she works. I'm sure wherever it is, the owners wouldn't mind a rockstar hanging around, even if it was only to stalk one of the staff. Grabbing my keys off the table, I make my way to the label before I end up doing something stupid.

I drop by Eddie's and pick him up on the way. He knows something is up but I'm not willing to share Melody with anyone, so I haven't opened up to him yet. It's not like me to keep something from him but I don't want him to judge me. He knows everything that is going on with Gabby, which has been a great help but I'm still not ready to open up.

We've barely said two words to each other when we arrive, but this isn't unusual. This lets me know Eddie has something going on and he needs a minute to get his head around it. This I can totally sympathize with.

Watching the music video again is as painful as I expected but it had to be done, otherwise, people would think something is wrong. As we sign the paperwork, we see the other three haven't signed yet.

"Logan, you need to tell the boys about Gabby." Eddie's comment catches me off guard.

"What makes you say that man?" He takes in a deep breath whilst contemplating his reply.

"Dumb and dumber haven't got a clue about relationships." That's Eddie's pet name for Cody and Hunter, "They don't respect marriage and everything that comes with it but Spencer... He cares about Gabby. He needs to hear from you what's going on. How do you think he would feel if he found out from someone else? Or worse, the tabloids?"

"Who else would tell him? The tabloids don't even know I'm married so how the fuck would they find out? As for someone else telling him, only a few people know what's going on, so who would do it? Unless you plan on telling him?" Eddie looks at me with a look of disgust.

"You know damn well that I wouldn't do that. And if you actually think that then you're a bloody idiot mate." When Eddie gets fired up, his English accent gets stronger. I stifle a laugh at how ridiculous he sounds to me but it's too late. He smiles, knowing what he's done. "Oh, piss off, you wanker." He's laughing himself as soon as he's finished talking. That's the great thing about Eddie. He may be serious with his words, but our friendship goes beyond this band. He knows me better than anyone and even though I haven't told him about Melody, he knows that something is up.

"You're right though, man. I will tell them when the time is right." And just like that, we are good again. He knows better than anyone that this situation is killing me, but Gabby doesn't want people knowing so I have to respect her wishes for now.

We finish at the label a lot earlier than I had hoped and Eddie has other plans, so I am left on my own again. With nothing but thoughts of Melody, plaguing my mind. I never really understood addiction, but if my feelings are anything to go by, I've got a whole heap of sympathy for anyone who's ever had to battle it. Melody has quickly become my addiction and I'm already craving my next fix.

THIRTEEN

MELODY

G etting woken up by Avery jumping up and down on my bed was not how I thought my day would start, but here we are.

"Today is the day Melody Grace. Today is the day that the entire world gets to see you and the mighty fine Logan Pierce getting it on."

Her words confuse me at first. I still haven't told her anything yet but as I look at her face, with the big goofy smile spread across it, I realize what she must mean.

The music video.

I fear her wake-up call would've been a lot different if she knew what happened on set. Trouble is, her words still aren't entirely wrong, we did get it on a bit on set. A shiver creeps up my spine at the thought and echoes through a part of me that shouldn't feel like this whilst my best friend is laying on top of me.

"What are you on about, Ree?" She rolls off and places her head on the pillow next to me, bringing us face to face.

"The music video is being aired today. I had an email this morning, letting me know."

Tonight? She usually gets a bit more notice than this, what's the hurry?

"Oh, okay."

"Is that all you've got to say? Oh, okay? I thought that you would be as excited as I am. I feel like today is gonna drag. It's not airing until 8pm and I fear the wait might actually kill me."

Avery Moone, as dramatic as ever.

"Don't be silly, Ree."

With that, she jumps off my bed and leaves me on my own. I check my phone to see if maybe Logan had text me to let me know himself, but nothing. Rolling over, I try to go back to sleep but I know it isn't gonna happen. Not with everything that is going through my mind.

I've got ten hours to try and kill as quickly as possible. Actually, make that eleven because if this video looks anything like it felt on the day, I'm going to get some very awkward questions directed my way from Avery. I get up and sort myself out before I have to deal with Avery's fangirling again. By the time I finish doing my hair, I hope I've managed to at least kill two hours, but it turns out that it doesn't take me that long to get ready. One hour to be exact and I was taking my time. Making my way downstairs into the kitchen, I notice Avery is nowhere to be seen. So, I use this opportunity to flee the house, without even having my morning coffee. Grabbing my bag and keys I quietly sneak out to my car. I know that turning the engine on may alert Avery of my intentions but I'm not going to get anywhere by just sitting in the damn thing. So, I start the engine and drive off as quickly as I can. I'm not even thirty seconds down the road before my phone starts ringing. I ignore it as I know it is Avery, and I also know that she is going to ask me where I'm going. This way, I don't have to lie because honestly, I haven't got a fucking clue. I just know that I need to be away from her before the guilt gets the better of me and I end up telling her everything. I've become a pro at avoiding her recently. Fear has kept me away from her. Fear of telling her. Fear of her reaction. Fear of her reaching out to Gabriella. I will tell her, soon, but just not today, I tell myself again.

My day was wasted away mainly by shopping. I didn't buy anything, but I did finally make it to the salon to get my nails done. And even though I didn't need it yet, I took myself off to have a wax. I regretted that decision quickly enough.

Trying to kill more time, I make my way over to the club so that I can ask Barry if I can start an hour later tonight. Avery would never forgive me if I skipped out on her altogether and didn't watch the video with her. It's what we do. She gets a role in anything, we watch it together. Barry is nowhere to be seen out the front, so I go to his office. Hearing his voice confirms he's there so I push open the door, expecting him to be on the phone as it wasn't shut.

"Melody, what are you doing here?"

He shoots out of his chair like a man with a guilty conscience. But before he can get to me, the man he is having a meeting with, stands up and offers his hand,

"Hey darlin', I'm Troj. Nice to meet you." My hand is in his before I register.

"Troj? What kind of a name is that?" I regret the words as soon as they leave my mouth, but it doesn't seem to bother him one bit. His lips brush against my hand as Barry grabs hold of me,

"It's not a name you need to know right now. I've already spoken to Avery and you're off tonight. I'll speak to you tomorrow, okay?" Nodding, I can't take my eyes off this man in Barry's office. He is beautiful but it's not that. I can sense a darkness in him, something forbidden. He smirks and winks at me as Barry ushers me out, closing the door on me as soon as I'm past the threshold.

By the time I get in my car to head home, I chance a look at my phone. I've got fifty-six missed calls from Avery and a few angry texts. I choose to ignore them and just deal with this when I see her face to face. Stupidly, I thought that I might've had a message from Logan but maybe, because he has done this so many times before, it just isn't that big a deal for him.

Walking through my front door at 7.50pm was a pretty shitty thing to do. But so has everything I've done today. The day has really dragged but it's also been laced with fear. Fear over what Avery is going to say or do. As I turn into the sitting room, I'm face to face with an angry-looking Avery

"For fuck's sake, Melody Grace, I thought that you were gonna miss it. I can't believe that you abandoned me like that." She places her hands on her hips and lets out an exasperated sigh.

"I'm sorry, I'm just nervous. I didn't know how to deal with it, so I decided that I would be best on my own. This is all new to me. You're used to this sort of attention Ree, I'm not. I did the only thing that felt right and went out to try and take my mind off it." She lets out another sigh and then wraps her arms around me.

"It's a good job I love you, Dee. But please, don't ever do this to me again."

Her statement is completely wasted on me as I don't ever plan on being in this position, ever again.

"Never again, Ree. I promise."

Ushering me into the living room, I can see that she has set up our traditional selection of snacks and wine. I wasn't expecting this because of how mad she was at me, but I guess love wins this one. Taking off my coat, I go and hang it up before taking my usual seat in the living room.

I'm starting to feel sick at the thought of what happened between me and Logan on set being out there for the world to see.

I'm not one of those girls who jumps into bed with any guy who looks my way. Normally, I'm very cautious and I like to get to know people before letting my guard down. Or my pants, in this case. There was something about Logan though, much more than the way he looks. We just clicked instantly and everything that happened felt right. The electricity between us was off the charts, and it still is. I hate myself for feeling this way, especially now that I know he's married. To one of my friends, no less. I can't help how I feel and I'm starting to hate myself because of it.

Before I get lost in my thoughts, Avery comes running in with our wine glasses.

"I'm so excited Dee. I can't wait to see your face plastered everywhere. I know you weren't happy about the wardrobe, but I also knew that if I told you, you would've never agreed to do it. Please don't hate me. You're gonna be famous bitch, stop looking so worried."

Little does she know it isn't the thought of any fame that I am worried about. The thought of seeing my face as I orgasm is terrifying. Who really wants to see that, apart from a porn director? Oh God, I've accidentally made myself into a porn star. Downing my glass of wine, I grab the bottle and top it back up before the clock strikes 8pm.

"Dee dee, snap yourself out of it, it's about to air." I look at the screen, full of concern as to what we are about to witness. Hugging a cushion close to my chest, I take another gulp of wine in the hope that it might get me drunk enough not to care anymore.

The next five minutes go past in a haze of Guilty Pleasure. I feel relief like I've never felt before. They left in the scene in bed where the 'o' takes place, but they've somehow managed to make it look beautiful. They've also somehow managed to make me look beautiful. The chemistry between me and Logan was just as passionate and intense to watch as I remember it being on the day.

"Holy fucking shit, Melody. I think I just came in my panties a bit. I mean, that was sexy as fuck. I can't believe I was sick. I also can't believe you didn't tell me just how sexy that was." Relief washes over me. I've been worrying all day about this and how it would turn out.

"I can't believe it myself, Ree. That was...intense." Avery jumps up and starts frantically dancing around the room. She collapses in a heap next to me as we both laugh. She gives me a massive hug and that's when I see my phone is ringing,

"I need to go and answer my phone, Ree, it might be important."

"It might be Hollywood calling." She giggles as I scoop up my phone from the table. Making my way to my room, I see Logan is video calling me. Pushing my door closed, I take a glance in the mirror before answering

"Hey Logan, you okay?"

"Hey doll. I'm so sorry that I haven't contacted you sooner, I've been doing interviews at our label's office all day, promoting the single and I haven't had a minute. Have you seen it yet? I would've loved to see your face when you watched it."

Feeling my face starting to heat up, the wine gave me the courage I needed at this moment.

"Oh God, Logan, it was perfect. I've been worried all day about it if I'm honest. With what happened between us in the one scene, I thought I was about to launch my porn career, but it looked beautiful. Sexy even." He smiles shyly and I can feel my cheeks burning now.

"It really is perfect, isn't it?! You looked amazing. You look amazing, doll. I have to go as my phone is blowing up with messages. I'm on my way back now. The office is only twenty minutes or so away. So, hopefully I'll get to see you soon."

I'm not sure if he wants a straight answer to that but I go with what feels right. "Maybe, we'll see if I can fit you in sometime. What, with being in a rock video, I expect my phone to start *blowing up* any minute." I smile and blow him a kiss as he ends the call. Wow, that wine really has gone to my head.

Now that I have stopped, I feel wiped out. All the worry I've been carrying has finally caught up with me. The guilt still weighs heavy but all I can do is take Logan at his word and trust him. Knowing Avery would likely kill me if I went to bed now, I make my way back into the living room to try and enjoy the rest of the evening with my best friend.

FOURTEEN

MELODY

My head hates me.

My eyes hate me.

My mouth hates me.

My throat hates me.

My stomach hates me.

In fact, my whole body hates me.

All I can hear is a pounding in my ears. I put the pillow over my head in the hope that it will chase the noise away. Hearing the pounding again, I realize that it isn't in my head. Someone is at the front door. I get out of bed as quickly as I physically can, which isn't all that quickly. That's when I realize I'm completely naked. Grabbing my dressing gown, I slip it on as I make my way to the door. I hope it's no one important as I don't want to talk to anyone right now. Edging the door open, I swear I'm blinded as the sun beams through the gap.

"Morning doll. I brought you a strong coffee, a bacon

sandwich and some painkillers. I didn't know if you had any."
Oh, sweet baby Jesus, it had to be Logan, didn't it? I step away
from the door and let him in. Normally I wouldn't let anyone see
me in this state, but I hurt too much to care.

Pointing towards the kitchen, because that's about all I can
manage, I follow him as he leads the way, being sure to grab two
plates before sitting down. The sound of the plates rubbing
together makes my head feel like it's gonna pop. He hands over
the bacon sandwich with the hint of a smirk but given my state, I
don't challenge him. Manners be damned as I devour the
sandwich like an animal, whilst Logan watches on with an
amused expression. As soon as I swallow down the last bit, I
take a big swig of coffee and place my head on the table in the
hope it will ease the pain.

Twenty minutes pass without a single word but I feel my
head starting to clear. When I finally brave lifting my head, I
look across to Logan and see him smiling at me. It's only then
that something occurs to me.

"How did you know I'd need painkillers this morning? I
didn't tell you that I was having a drink last night." He chuckles
to himself as he replies.

"Maybe you should check your phone when I go." And he
winks at me. Oh God, what have I done? Grabbing the plates
from the table, I stand up and make my way to the sink. I feel
how red my face is going as I rack my brain, trying to
remember anything from last night. Everything got a bit fuzzy
after 10pm when the tequila came out. This right here is the
exact reason why I don't normally drink. I do stupid things and
I suffer for it too much the next day. Standing at the sink with
my head hanging, I can't bring myself to turn around and face
Logan. Especially when I finally realize what dressing gown I
have on. It is probably the worse one I could have picked up.
It's a very fluffy, very short leopard-print dressing gown that
Avery got me last Christmas. It's one thing wearing it in front of

Avery but something entirely different wearing it in front of someone else. Especially when I haven't got anything on underneath. Lifting my head, I shrug my shoulders and think, fuck it. I can't change anything that happened yesterday, so I may as well accept it. Bracing myself, I turn around to face Logan, but he isn't at the table. He's standing right in front of me.

"Sorry Logan, for everything. I don't know what I sent you but whatever it is, I'm sorry." He grabs both my arms gently and starts stroking them up and down.

"It's okay, doll. There's no point looking at your phone. You video called me at midnight, that's all. You said hi, told me that we looked hot in the video and then fell asleep. It was actually kinda cute." On one hand, I feel relieved, knowing that it could've been so much worse but on the other hand, I'm embarrassed I did it. I place my forehead on his chest and start laughing. I'm not sure why I'm laughing but I can't stop myself. Logan starts laughing as well and before I know it, we are both shedding tears of laughter. I cover my face with my hands and lean into his chest once more. He wraps his arms around me and his laughter ricochets through me. We stay like this for what feels like an eternity but in reality, it's only a minute. I remove my hands from my face and lift my head. It's then I realize I can't take a step back as I'm against the sink. Logan's hands drop down to my waist and he lowers his eyes to meet mine. The moment feels almost too intense, I can feel my heart speeding up more and more with each passing second.

Under my hands I feel his heart beating, strong and steady. My breathing feels almost labored, he steals my breath away with his icy gaze. Goosebumps break out across my whole body as he leans forward, touching my nose with his. At this moment, nothing else exists. Just me and him, breathing the same air, sharing the same space. This is the most intense moment of my life and I make a mental note to remember what this feels like, right now. Butterflies going crazy in my lower stomach like nothing I've ever felt before.

The moment is broken by the sound of Avery screeching.

"Holy shit. Logan Pierce is in my fucking kitchen."

My head drops as Logan steps away, raising his hands in the air. Looking up, I see Avery standing in the doorway with armfuls of groceries and a look of fangirling confusion across her face. Logan grabs a bag from under her arm, placing it on the table.

"Avery, I assume. Nice to meet you at last." He holds out his hand for her to shake as she puts down the rest of the bags, nodding her head. No words leave her lips as she stares at him some more, completely starstruck. Turning to me, he makes his escape.

"I should go. I'll speak to you soon doll and arrange to take Oz and Zach to the park again."

He winks and disappears out of the front door as quickly as he arrived. I turn to look at Avery and she looks more confused than ever.

"How does he know my name? He's supposed to think that you're Avery. And why the heck would he want to take Zach and Ozzy out?" I see the wheels turning in Ree's head, so I start at the easiest point.

"He knows I'm not you, Ree." I see the questions on the tip of her tongue, "And he wants to take the boys out because... He's Ozzy's Dad." Shock resonates through her the same way it did with me. The only difference here is, she hasn't done anything wrong. Closing my eyes, I hear the break in her voice the moment she figures it out.

"That means he's... but you two were just about to... what the fuck, Dee? Is he Gabriella's husband?" She already knows the answer to this. I can see when I look in her eyes that she recognizes my guilt. Turning my back to her, I brace myself on the sink for the tongue lashing she is about to give me. Moments pass without a word and I hang my head in shame as the tears slowly trickle out. To my surprise, she wraps her arms around me and takes a deep breath.

"I can't lie, Dee, this is a lot to take in. I don't know what the heck is going on and why. But I know you well enough to know there is a legit reason you haven't told me." Taking her hands in mine, I turn around to face her.

"It's such a mess Ree. I wanted to talk to you, but I didn't know where to start." She lets go of my hands and makes her way over to the coffee machine.

"We've got a few hours before I have to pick Zach up. So, I'm gonna make us a drink whilst you catch me up on everything, okay?" Grabbing a tissue, I wipe the tears away as I agree. This is the moment I've dreaded, but I also know that I need her if I'm to make any sense of this situation.

FIFTEEN

MELODY

That's exactly what I spend the next three hours doing. I know Avery is pissed off with me for a number of different reasons, but she is hiding it well. We've been best friends for longer than I care to remember, and I understand why she's mad at me. I think she's letting it go for now because she can see I'm punishing myself enough for the both of us. I make myself a big mug of coffee as she leaves to go and get Zach and lock myself in my room. I'm emotionally worn out now and feel like I could sleep for a week. Exhausted, I flop down onto my bed and that's when I see my phone on my bedside cabinet. I can see the light is flashing, indicating that I have a message. I'm in two minds whether or not I want to look at it but, I know it will start to annoy me if I don't. Leaning across, I grab my phone and I see a missed call and a message from Logan.

Hey doll, I'm sorry I ran out on you earlier. I hope you didn't

*come under too much fire from Avery. I'll make it up to you,
promise.*

Too drained to deal with this, I decide to not reply and get my
head down for an hour instead. I've got work tonight and I don't
think Barry would be impressed if I had another night off.
Although, I'm sure at the moment he would be happy not having
to pay my wages.

I woke up later than planned, I must have slept through my
alarm. I barely have time to get dressed and brush my teeth
before I'm rushing to my car.

Avery avoided me as I rushed around downstairs, trying to
get my shit together. Normally she helps me, even has it ready
for me sometimes, but not today. That's okay though, I can cope
with this. It's much better than her shouting at me before I leave
for work. I've cried enough for one day. She's probably thinking
of all the ways she can punish me for my bad behavior or
something. So silence I can deal with.

Work was slow tonight. This was the last thing I needed as it
gave me too much time to think. I hate that it's like this for two
reasons.

One, I hate seeing Barry in any kind of trouble, and this is
starting to get very serious for him.

Two, it drags when we haven't got the punters in to keep us
busy. We had another girl who didn't turn up to work tonight. It
sucks but on the plus side, it's wages that don't need to be paid. I

had another look at the books tonight before I left and it's not looking good. I've suggested to Barry that maybe we should close earlier on weekdays, but he isn't having it. Not yet anyway.

I don't arrive home until nearly 4am. The lights are all off in the house, which is a good sign that Avery's still mad at me. She normally leaves the porch light on for me. Letting myself in, I go straight to my room, dropping my bag on my bed as I go to the bathroom and brush my teeth. A shower would be good right now, but it can wait till morning. That is the one plus side of not being busy, I'm not covered in beer from over-excited punters. Stripping out of my clothes, I take my phone from my bag as I get into bed. That's when I see a missed call from Logan. I completely forgot to message him back earlier and I don't think he'd appreciate a call at this early hour. Setting an alarm, I name it 'message Logan' so that I don't forget again.

I wake to the sound of my alarm, slightly surprised by the fact that Zach wasn't the one to wake me this morning. Yet again, it's another sign of Avery's anger. Leaning over, I grab my phone to turn off the alarm. That's when I see the message I left for myself. Before I overthink it, I text Logan.

Hey Logan. Sorry I didn't respond yesterday, things didn't go well and then I had work. I'm sure Avery will be okay soon, she just needs a minute to wrap her head around everything. Hope you're good.

Throwing my phone onto my bed, I go and take a shower. Normally I would put music on as I get ready, but I give it a miss today. I don't want to give Avery any more reasons to be mad at me.

Finishing up, I make my way back to my bedroom in time to hear my phone ringing. I see that it's Logan calling, and I answer it quickly before Avery hears. I know that I'm overthinking this, but I can't help it. I made a mistake by sleeping with him in the first place. Now I feel guilty just thinking about him. I suppose you could say that he has become my Guilty Pleasure.

"Hello."

"Hey doll, you okay? Sorry to hear that things didn't go well with Avery."

"It's okay. She just needs some time. Is everything okay with you?"

"Well yes but I need your help. I wouldn't normally ask but I'm out of options."

"What is it?"

"Any chance that you could have Ozzy for me tonight? He should be at his Grandparents, but something came up. I have some band stuff that I have to do, and I've been told there will be hell to pay if I don't turn up."

"Oh no. I'm working tonight but I can ask Avery if you want? She may be angry with me, but she would never let Zach suffer for my sins."

"Oh shit, do you think she'd mind?"

"It should be fine, I'll let you know."

"Okay, thanks, doll. Only if you're sure though."

"It's all good. I'll message you as soon as I've spoken to her."

"Speak to you soon, beautiful."

"Bye."

I try to ignore the fact he just called me beautiful but it's all that I can think about. Sitting in a daydream for a good five minutes before I remember that I'm supposed to be asking Avery about having Ozzy.

I find her in the kitchen, cleaning.

"Hey Ree, can I, well Logan, ask you a favor?" She swings around and glares at me,

"Yes Dee. What would you, or should I say Logan, like to ask me?" She is definitely still mad.

"Is there any chance you could have Ozzy tonight? He's supposed to be with his Grandparents, but something come up. I would have him myself, but I have to work tonight. I wouldn't normally ask, but…"

"It's okay, Dee, you don't have to think up excuses for him, I'll have him. But only because Zach would love it." I knew she'd have him because of Zach. Those boys love each other.

"What time shall I tell Logan to drop him off?"

"Say around Four. I would offer to pick him up from school, but I need to run some errands. It's hard enough doing it with Zach, I don't fancy doing it with both of them."

"Thank you, Ree. I'll let him know." I turn to walk away but before I manage to take a step, Avery stops me.

"Just a little FYI, Dee. I saw Gabriella this morning and she looked awful. I hope to God it's not because she's just found out that her husband cheated on her. I know you didn't know when you slept with him, but you do now. I think it would be best if you took a step back. Gabriella doesn't deserve that." I don't know what to say to her, so I just nod my head and make my way back into my room. This is all too much to take in before having my morning coffee but after that scolding from Avery, I decide it's best to leave her to it. I text Logan the time to drop off Ozzy and he replies with a simple thank you.

Avoiding Avery for as long as possible seems like the best thing I can do today. So, I clean my room like a scolded child. I don't think I have ever spent so much time in my room since we moved in. My bathroom is so clean you could eat your dinner off the floor, and I don't think I have ever organized my closet as well in my whole life. Looking at the time, I see that Avery should've left to pick up Zach, so I go and make myself the coffee that I've been jonesing for.

After two cups and something to eat, I make my way back into my room to start getting myself ready for work. I take another shower, as I am feeling grubby after cleaning everything.

Wrapping my hair in a towel, I make quick work of drying myself off and throw on my dressing gown. No point in getting dressed until after I have done my hair and make-up. Drying off my hair, I've got time to curl it instead of straightening. As I am plugging my curling irons in, there is a knock on my bedroom door. I'm surprised to see Avery on the other side of the door.

"Hey Dee, can you just keep an ear out for Zach? I have to go back to the shop as I forgot something. He's asleep in his room, so he shouldn't be any bother." Stunned by the fact that she knocked and asked, instead of barging in and telling me, I nod my head and respond.

"Yes. Of course I can." She gives me a small smile and whispers a thank you as she walks away. Thankfully, I have the day off tomorrow so I can try and make this up to her and show her how sorry I really am. I take a seat back at my vanity table and start doing my hair.

I finish my hair in no time and move on to my make-up. Just as I finish applying my foundation there's a knock at the front door. Glancing at the clock, as I make my way out of my room and that's when I see that it is just gone 4pm, so it must be Logan with Ozzy. I open the door and let them both in. Ozzy pulls me down for a hug before running off into Zach's room. I look up at Logan to see him smiling.

"That boy of mine really loves you guys. It's all he has spoken about since I picked him up."

Noticing the smell of burning, I remember that I didn't turn my curling iron off. I go running off into my room, leaving Logan at the door. Thankfully, there isn't much damage done.

It looks like I accidentally threw my makeup sponge on them and it was about to catch fire.

Taking them into my bathroom, I place them in the sink. When I return to my room, Logan is standing in the doorway.

"Everything okay, doll?"

Not knowing what to say, I nod as I walk back over to my vanity table. I think I'm in shock as I start to tidy the new mess I have created, worrying about what could have happened. Logan places his hand on my arm, and it makes me jump a little as I turn round.

Before I say anything, his lips land on mine. Running his tongue across my bottom lip, I shudder. Gently, he opens his mouth and I allow his tongue to connect with mine. The kiss almost feels lazy as we slowly make out.

He raises his hand and places it on my neck. As he does this, he starts to speed up the movement of his tongue. Placing his other hand on my waist he pushes me into my dresser. I don't know if it was the impact of the dresser on my ass or not, but suddenly I'm reminded how wrong this is.

Putting my hand on his chest, I use it to push him away.

"We can't do this, Logan. It's wrong."

"Why does it feel so right then, doll?" He goes to make another move on me as I stand back up straight, so I push him away harder this time.

"You're married, Logan. You may be okay doing this to your wife, but I'm not." His demeanor changes in an instant.

"You have no fucking idea about my fucking wife, Melody." He turns to walk away, and I can't hold it in any longer.

"You might make a habit of doing this, Logan Pierce, but I don't. What I've done is fucking breaking me. Gabriella is my friend. I can't do this now I know she's your wife. Those vows may have meant nothing to you but my friendship with her means something to me. She is one of my closest friends and I actually love her." He starts laughing a manic laugh as he responds.

"If she was that close of a friend then you would be more clued up about her. She has secrets, Melody. Secrets that will break your heart. Don't tell me that you love her, like I don't. You haven't got a fucking clue. It breaks my heart when I have to look at her every day, knowing what I know but not able to say a word to anyone. I'm fucking done with this shit. Thank Avery for me. I will be back in the morning to get Ozzy. I hope you have a long and happy fucking life Melody Grace and I hope you never have to go through what I'm going through now." He storms out of my room and a few seconds later I hear the front door slam.

Unable to hold back the tears, I fall into my chair and let them fall freely.

Knowing that we were never meant to be doesn't mean this doesn't hurt. We were never going to be more than we are right now, but I can't help but feel like I've just lost a piece of my heart.

The tears take over as my mind wanders to Gabriella. How could I be falling for her husband? What kind of shitty friend would do that?

Avery comes storming into my room and throws her arms around me.

"I'm so sorry Dee, I heard all of that. You did the right thing ya know." I know she is right. I know it was the right thing to do but that doesn't make it hurt any less.

"I know Ree. It just hurts. I feel things for him that I know I shouldn't, but I can't help it." She hugs me in tighter and gives me a final squeeze before getting up and making her way out.

"You may be hurting now Dee but just think about how much Gabriella is gonna hurt if she ever found out." Her words stung like a mother fucker, but she is only telling the truth. Gabriella would be devastated, I'm sure.

Turning to look in the mirror, I hate the person looking back at me. The mascara and red blotches all over my face make me think that I should probably re-do my makeup.

Thankfully, by the time I get to my eyes, the swelling has gone down, and the tears have stopped falling.

I can feel myself going numb. This is probably a good thing as it means that I'm finally flushing out any unwanted feelings for him.

Pushing everything to the back of my mind, I apply a bit more makeup than normal. Anything to help me feel even a tiny bit better. Putting on my favorite underwear, a bright orange bra, and panties, I get into my uniform and pray for a busy night.

Being sure to say goodbye to Avery and the boys before I go, I jump in my car and make the short drive to work. Although I know it's a short drive, it seemed even shorter tonight as I pulled up outside the club. Taking a deep breath, I make my way inside.

SIXTEEN

LOGAN

I'm fucking raging as I leave Melody. What fucking right has she got to use my wife against me? She hasn't got a fucking clue about anything. She even had the nerve to insinuate that I make a habit out of this.

How. Fucking. Dare. She.

If she thinks this is breaking her now, then she is in for a big shock soon enough. If she loves Gabby as much as she says, then the next time she sees her is going to rip her fucking heart out. I was hoping to save her from some of the pain. Try to be there for her if she needed me but fuck her. She can deal with this on her own now, I'm out.

Jumping into my car I decide to go straight to the club to meet the boys. I was planning on dropping it off at home and getting a taxi, but I need a fucking drink ASAP. I can worry about my car tomorrow.

Arriving earlier than planned, I lock up and head towards the club. Just before I get to the door I look up, finally noticing the hideous sign. It looks like some kind of 80's throwback with its bright neon pink lettering glaringly spelling out 'The Cherry Pickers'. Right next to it, in the same pink neon, is the silhouette of a woman with cherries for an ass. What the fuck was Cody thinking suggesting a shithole like this? I've never liked going out to clubs, but I reluctantly agreed tonight because of how insane life is for all of us. We need this time together to let loose. It's also an ideal time to take Eddie's advice and talk to the boys about Gabby. Given everything that's been happening lately, I would've probably blown off tonight, but I worry this is the last chance I'll have to tell them before everything kicks off with the band again and this isn't a conversation I wanna have with a record label dogs body hanging around us.

Let's just hope this place isn't as hideous inside.

Pushing my way through the door and heading straight to the bar I see that it isn't bad inside, it looks okay. I mean, it's not the fucking Ritz but if I wanted that, I would have gone there. Ordering myself a shot of Crystal Skull, I throw it down my neck as soon as the bartender stops pouring, signaling for another. I'm not usually a big drinker but I'm willing to do anything that'll help me forget the last hour. Digging my card out of my back pocket, I hand it over to the bartender. This is gonna get messy so it's easier for everyone if he just opens us a tab. Just as I indicate for the next one someone slaps me on the shoulder.

"Make that four, bar keep. And four bottles of beer to follow. We are on it tonight lads" without looking, I already know that it's Spencer. Hard to mistake him with that English accent that the ladies love so much.

"What's up guys" We all share a quick man-hug as Cody, Hunter, and Spencer down their shots.

Looking over to Eddie, I signal to see if he wants a water. This could be a long night for him being the only one of us that doesn't drink.

"Let's take our drinks and get a table." Eddie pipes up. Being sober has never made him a killjoy but I'm sure he doesn't want us at the bar all night getting fucked up. Also, the more alcohol Cody, Hunter, and Spenser consume, the sneakier they become. Practical jokes are not fun when you are on the receiving end of them.

The next hour flies by which is exactly what I needed. I'm still mad about what happened earlier with Melody but this time with the boys is really helping to take the edge off.

Hunter signals over to the bar for another round and is greeted with a thumbs up from the bartender, Barry. As I turn back round, I see Cody staring off into the distance.

"Seen something you like, Code?" He shakes his head a little.

"I'm sure I recognize that waitress from somewhere. I can't put my finger on it though." Spencer leans round to get a better look.

"You probably fucked her at some stage or another. I mean, you were the one who suggested this dive."

"No, that's not it. Trust me, dude, I would remember hitting that fine piece of ass. Fuck. This is really starting to piss me off now."

I can't help but laugh at the utter confusion on his face. He has fucked so many women, it would be a miracle if he remembered one, so I wouldn't be at all surprised if he had fucked this waitress. All of a sudden, he looks straight at me, smirks, and then sits bolt upright. I can see the waitress putting our drinks down out of the corner of my eye, but I can't stop watching Cody and his ever-changing emotions.

"Well, hey there beautiful. Can I just say, I think you looked amazing in our music video. But in the flesh, you are just fucking stunning." It couldn't be. Could it? I turn just in time to see Melody looking like a rabbit caught in headlights.

"Melody? What the fuck? You don't seriously work *here*?"

"Melody? I thought her name was Avery?" Cody looks even

more confused now. It seems like a lifetime ago all that shit happened. I forgot the rest of the guys didn't know.

"Seriously, doll, you never mentioned that you worked here. Why didn't you tell me?" She looks me dead in the eyes and says through gritted teeth.

"Probably because it is none of your business Logan. And anyway, you never asked." I go to respond but I realize she's right. I never fucking asked her once where she worked. I knew that she did work, obviously, but I never took the time to ask her where. As I sit here, feeling like a selfish dick, I notice her uniform. Or lack of it. That's when I remember the conversation that we had about her uniform and her saying about how tight it was. Well, she wasn't fucking wrong. It leaves very little to the imagination that's for sure. A black skin-tight vest with the words "cherry pickers" right across her tits and shorts that might as well not be on. They are so fucking short it's unreal. All I can focus on right now is her legs. She has got the most perfectly formed, long legs. I remember what they felt like wrapped around my head while I feasted on her glorious pussy. I look up and notice she's scowling at me, but I can't help but smirk. Cody stands up and makes his way next to Melody. He leans over and tries to whisper in her ear but I'm close enough to hear every word he says.

"So, how much for a piece of you then babe?" She recoils in horror but handles herself perfectly.

"I'm not for sale, babe, but even if I were, I'm pretty sure that I'm way out of your price range." Picking up the empties she saunters away, leaving Cody open-mouthed and me as hard as a fucking rock. We all burst out laughing, it's not often Cody is left speechless. As the laughter dies down, I grab the opportunity to readjust myself before anyone notices.

The night carries on pretty much the same, with Melody as our waitress but now she is completely ignoring me. I've tried to speak to her numerous times, but she shoots me down with a fake ass smile and some sarcastic reply. I know the rest of the guys can sense the tension between us but none of them have the balls to say anything to me yet.

———

All the alcohol has made its way to my bladder and it's time to break the seal. Making my way to the restroom, Hunter stands and starts to walk with me, but he deviates toward the bar, probably spotting his next victim.

As I'm standing at the urinal, I hear someone clearing their throat behind me. Looking in the mirror, I see that it's a woman, twirling her hair whilst looking me up and down.

"Can I help you, love?"

This is a good indication that I have had enough to drink, I'm starting to sound like Spencer.

"I noticed you the moment you walked in." Her eyes are all kinds of fucked up and I'm guessing she's high right now. I shake off, zip up, and turn round to face her.

"Look, love, no offence but I'm just trying to have a quiet night out with my friends. Is there anything I can actually do for you? You are aware that you're in the men's room right now?" She isn't wearing much. Just a corset and a tiny skirt. She takes a step towards me and places her hand on my chest.

"I would get the sack if my boss knew I was doing this, but we don't often get the lookers like you in here. For that reason, I'll make you a deal. Anything you want for half the price." She leans in, trying to kiss me but I take a step back before she manages to connect. She wobbles on her feet, but it only takes a heartbeat for her to correct herself.

"Oh, come on, big boy, let me see that big, hard dick of yours. I'll make it good for you, promise." I have no doubt in my mind that most men would happily take her up on her offer, but I could think of nothing worse right now. She is out of her fucking mind, fucked up on drugs and that shit right there just makes me fucking mad.

"Look lady, I don't wanna offend ya here but hell no. You need to sort your shit out." She looks up at me with hazy eyes.

"Okay, man, just don't tell my boss. He'll try and put me in rehab or some shit. I ain't got time for that." She then shrugs her shoulders, turns around, and walks out, probably to find some other John who will pay her for her next fix. I make a mental note to have a word with her boss before I leave. I exit the men's room as fast as my legs can carry me and head straight over to our table, noticing that Hunter isn't back yet, so I glance over to the bar to see if he is there. Sure enough, he is there propping up the bar, looking like he's doing some kind of shady deal. He's talking to the big guy with broad shoulders and short dark hair. Barry, I think his name is, and another guy who reminds me of a Viking from a show I've been watching about a kingdom.

As I take a seat at the table, Cody leans over to me.

"Rumor has it that you can get whatever you want if you're willing to pay the right price. I've heard stories about the different rooms in the back. Apparently, they have different rooms for different tastes." He winks as he leans back towards Spencer. "Why d'you think I wanted to meet here, dude." The thought of Melody working in a place like this gets my blood boiling. I know she said she was a waitress, but you can't tell me that every red-blooded man hasn't looked at her and thought about trying their luck. I mean, she is fucking stunning. She is everything that a man could ever want in a woman. She has curves in all the right places. Shit, I've got to stop thinking about her like I am right now, I only just managed to hide it the last time. Looking up to take a look around at the boys and I can tell something is off. No one is speaking and they all look shifty as fuck. Spencer glances at me and looks away before I have a chance to question him. I look to Cody who pretty much does the same. Finally, I look at Eddie who just grimaces and shrugs his shoulders.

"What the fuck happened Eddie? What is Hunter up to? He's been at the bar for ages." Eddie looks at his feet, shrugging his shoulders.

"I don't know man. Knowing Hunter, he's probably trying to set Cody up with that bar dude." We all laugh at that because it's probably true.

That is the type of crazy shit these fuckers get up to when they're together. Thankfully they normally leave me and Eddie out of it. I think they mainly leave Eddie out of it because the last time they tried to get him involved, he knocked them all out. Never seen anything like it in my life. One punch, out cold. All three of them. Then he just sat down and lit a cigarette as if nothing happened. They were all absolutely fine but neither one of them has had the balls to mess with him since. I'm not totally sure why they have never got me involved though. Maybe it's because I spend most of my time with Eddie? I don't really care, I'm just glad that they don't involve me. Hunter comes walking back over with a huge shit-eating grin on his face. He looks me straight in the eyes and smiles, so I have to ask,

"What the fuck are you up to, man?" He winks at me,

"You'll find out soon enough, big guy." Oh fucking hell I think Eddie might be right after all. He takes a seat next to Spencer and whispers something in his ear. Then starts laughing and looks over towards Cody, flipping him the bird. A little time passes, and I notice Hunter constantly glancing at the bar. This time, he raises his arm signaling for another drink. Looking over myself in the hope of catching a glimpse of Melody.

We may not be talking right now but that doesn't mean I have to stop appreciating her. The woman walking towards us is definitely not Melody. It may be dark in here, but I would recognize Melody's figure anywhere. As she gets closer, I can see she is one of the dancers that was on stage earlier.

Normally I wouldn't even notice the dancer's face, but I found myself staring at their faces as they danced, instead of their bodies. I know this has a lot to do with Melody being here, but I don't know why I'm letting it affect me like this. Considering what happened earlier, I really shouldn't give a shit.

SEVENTEEN

MELODY

When I left for work earlier, I was hoping that I wouldn't see Logan ever again. Unfortunately for me, him and his bandmates decided to have a night at the Cherry Pickers. It is both a blessing and a curse that they happened to sit in my section. Getting to shut Logan down every time he tried to speak to me feels amazing. But, just seeing him is chipping away at me more and more. This night can't end soon enough. It's gone midnight as I get myself a drink from behind the bar. Barry doesn't mind me having the odd glass of wine, providing I don't get drunk. Just as I sit down and take a sip, Barry comes over.

"Can I have a word with you in the office please Dee?" His face looks serious as he turns and heads to the office, without waiting for me. Picking up my glass of wine, I make my way out the back. As I pass through the bar, I feel eyes on me. Only this time, it's not Logan. The guy from Barry's office the other day is propped up at the bar. His eyes meet mine and he raises his glass to me with a wink that would have most girls' panties dropping, downing his shot in one. The bartender is quick to refill as he places the glass down. The thought of Barry waiting in his office is the only thing that has me walking away. I don't know anything about him, but I feel his eyes can tell a thousand tales. This time, I knock on the door before walking in. Barry is sitting on his desk and shakes his head at me as I enter. Taking a seat, Barry puts his hands together, stopping and starting a few times before the words finally come out.

"We've had an offer of an insane amount of money for a girl to dance. No sex. No nakedness. Just dance." It's not the words I expected to hear when I stepped through the door.

"Exactly how insane is this offer, Barry?" Taking in a few deep breaths, he finally answers.

"Fifteen thousand dollars." I look at him, making sure I heard him right.

"Fifteen thousand dollars to just dance? What's the catch?" Barry's eyes fail to meet mine as he looks at the floor. He may have told me already that it's just to dance but who offers someone fifteen thousand dollars with no chance of a happy ending?

"They want you, Dee." A stunned silence fills the room. I don't know how to respond, "I've told them no." Our eyes lock and the shock I feel now is different.

"Why did you say no, Barry. You need this money." The words flow from my mouth before I think about who they have asked to dance for them. Me.

"Money isn't everything. You didn't sign up for this when you started working for me and I sure as hell ain't gonna make you do this." A sense of pride fills my heart.

"Who is the dance for?" Barry looks confused for a moment but soon gets his head back in the game.

"Some guy called Hunter? Came in with the one who's been watching you all night." My cheeks flush at the thought of anyone else noticing.

"So, it's not for Logan then?" Barry tries to play it off, but I can see he's not telling me something.

"Would it make a difference if it was?" I stop and think for a moment.

"Honestly Barry, I don't know. But for 15K I'm gonna give whoever it is the best damn dance I've ever given." Grabbing the bottle of Crystal Skull Vodka from Barry's desk, I pop the cork and take a big swig.

"Hey, that's meant to be for special occasions."

I look at Barry as I replace the lid. "If this isn't a fucking special occasion, then lord knows what is." Barry shrugs his shoulders as he pulls me in for a hug.

"This is gonna be the easiest five grand you've ever earnt." Breaking the hug, I look Barry in the eyes,

"I don't want a cent from this. I'm doing it to help the club…"

"I can't let you do that Dee."

"You have no choice, Barry. It's all yours. I don't want 5k from this as I'm doing it for you." Tears fill his eyes and I'm convinced he's about to cry.

"There's no point in trying to talk you out of it, is there." Finally, he gets it.

"No Barry. I do the books and I'll make sure it all goes to you whether you like it or not. But a new purse never goes amiss." I wink at him as I usher him out of the office. If I'm going to this then I need to get out of my uniform and put on something more suitable. Although Barry never confirmed it was Logan, everything in me knows that it probably is. I'm still really angry with him after what happened earlier and this has been one of the hardest nights for me, to date. Feeling as angry as I've felt but putting on a fake smile and pretending to be happy isn't me but there is no way I'm letting Logan win. He invades my thoughts in the moments I let my mind wander but tonight was the reality check I needed. This may be some kind of rockstar fling for him, but I know I'm already more invested than that. I don't just wanna be another notch on the bedpost or a cool story to tell their friends. I'm not the kind of girl who hits it and quits it, I want to be more than just a challenge to someone. I wanna be someone's everything. I wanna be the last thing they think of when they fall asleep at night and the first thing they think of when they open their eyes in the morning. I wanna be the beginning, the middle, and the end. I'm not gonna get that with Logan Pierce so I need to use this moment to get out.

Rummaging around the office, I find the clothes I need. Although the dancers don't have a uniform, Barry always makes sure he has certain clothes on hand at all times in case any of them need it. As I strip off my uniform, I catch a glimpse of myself in the mirror. I can't believe I'm about to do this. Slipping on the black mini skirt, it's much shorter than I thought it would be, but I guess that's what happens when you have an ass to fill it. The shirt only comes to just below my tits, so I tie it in a knot. I try to do up the buttons but give up on that quickly as my shaking hands won't grip them properly. One final glance in the mirror and I make my way out of the office and towards the back room.

I'm not sure if the buzz I feel is from the alcohol or nerves. As I stand in front of the door, I take one last shot from a miniature I stole from Barry's drawer. I take a moment to catch my breath and slow my breathing down. My heart races as I know who is waiting on the other side of the door, so I use this time to collect my thoughts and build a game plan in my head.

I need to know that I can walk in that room, do what I gotta do, and then walk out. Whatever this thing is with Logan ends tonight. When I walk out of that room, everything will be different.

EIGHTEEN

LOGAN

The woman in question stops right in front of me. That's when I see she doesn't have any drinks.

"Can I help you, darling?" She looks me up and down and smirks.

"I need you to come with me, *darling.*" The last thing I wanna do is shoot her down in front of all the boys and her work friends, but I'm not in the mood for this shit.

"I'm sorry, babe, but I don't feel like having a private dance from anyone tonight, yourself included. I'm just here to hang out with my boys, okay?" She looks around the guys, probably trying to figure out which one of them would be up for it. Then she laughs to herself as her eyes land back on me.

"I hate to be the one to break it to you, *babe*, but your boys are the ones who already paid for this. And just so you know, it's not me who will be dancing for you. We have got someone special lined up for you." She grabs my hand and winks at Cody as she drags me towards the back rooms, only giving me a second to flip the bird at the band. I'd love nothing more than to turn around and run away, to waste their money on something I never asked for. But no, fuck 'em. They're probably standing nearby, betting on how long it takes me to up and leave. Those shits know me well enough to know how much I hate this kinda thing. Which is exactly why I'm in this position. Turns out the joke was on me tonight.

I'm led into a dark purple room out the back, a large leather couch almost fills the back wall, which I'm taken to and signaled to have a seat. I hate to think just how many people have used this chair but on a positive note, it does smell and look surprisingly clean. I take a seat in the middle as the lady in question makes her way back out of the door. Just as she is pulling the door closed behind her, she peaks her head back in.

"I hope you enjoy yourself babe but be sure to follow the rules." Confused by her statement, I go to shout at her as she slams the door shut. That's when I see a list of rules stuck to the back of the door. They all seem like pretty standard rules. No touching the dancers, no added extras, if you make a mess then clean it up, and so on.

Leaning back in the seat, I finally take in my surroundings. A chest of drawers that has a black speaker on sits in one corner with nothing much else. A black framed mirror hangs on the badly painted wall to my left. Looking a bit closer, I try to see if there's any form of intercom around or something like a camera where they keep an eye on the girls. The more I look around the room, the more I feel my buzz fading. I'm not a big drinker and I know I've had more than enough tonight but with Melody as our waitress, I kept on ordering. Any excuse to have her near me. Good thing there was a bucket nearby as that's where some of my drinks went. If I'd drank everything I ordered, I'd be home by now.

Why in the hell did I agree to this? Well, I didn't exactly agree but I didn't put up a fight either. The thought of having some strange woman, who works with Melody, touching me is starting to make me feel a little uneasy. When I decided to come in here, a part of me did it to make Melody jealous. I wanted to see if she reacted to it, or even if she'd try and stop me. A part of me still wants her to come crashing through that door and beg me not to do this but I fear that will never happen. The more I think about this, the more uncomfortable I become.

Just as I motion to get up, the lights dim, and music starts playing from the speaker. Looking towards the door as it slowly opens, I begin to feel a bit sick thinking about what's about to happen. Leaning forward, I take a deep breath whilst focusing on the floor to prepare myself for what comes next. What red-blooded male dreads the thought of a practically naked woman putting on a show for him? I can't control the chill that runs down my spine, causing me to shake. I hope that whoever is entering the room, doesn't mistake my shakes for nervousness. Hearing the door close is the confirmation I needed to realize I can't do this. This is probably gonna be the easiest money this dancer has made in a long time, but I'm out. Looking up, with the words to tell her no on the tip of my tongue, the second my eyes hit hers I knew that I would never say no to her.

"Melody?" She breaks eye contact the moment her name leaves my lips, looking to the floor.

"What are you doing? I thought you said that you weren't a dancer here?" A million questions and doubts float around my head but all is lost when I see her take a deep breath and start walking over to me. I can't take my eyes off her. I don't think I will ever get enough of her, even if I had a whole lifetime to do so. She is wearing the tiniest skirt I've ever seen, with a white shirt that's tied in a knot under her tits with her bright orange bra on show, all wrapped up with a loose black tie. She looks fucking incredible but to be fair, she would look incredible in anything.

Stopping in front of me, it takes all my willpower not to reach out and touch her because I know one touch isn't enough and I don't think I have it in me to stop. She looks nervous as she chews on her bottom lip. What she doesn't realize is that one simple action has me wanting to shoot my load in my pants.

"Your band mates seem to have more money than sense. Thanks to them, this place just got the cash injection it needed." Raising my eyebrow, she pushes on my shoulder before I say anything, sending me back in the chair. Any response I had is lost as she slowly starts to move to the music, swaying her hips from side to side which has me in a trance as her hands expertly run up and down her body, removing her shirt as she goes. Turning around slowly, her ass is within reach and I've never wanted to grab and bite something so badly before. My mouth starts to water at the thought as she turns to face me once again. Leaning forward, she places her hands on either side of my head and I can't take my eyes off her tits as they dangle in front of me with nothing but a simple piece of material keeping them contained and out of full view. Placing her knees on the chair, either side of mine, I grip the chair tight. It's the only control I have right now as she lowers her ass onto my waiting lap. I worry that if I let go, I may never want to let go of her. Watching in awe as she runs her hands up her legs, the same legs that are now touching mine, lifting her skirt as she goes, fully revealing the bright orange panties that match her bra. Unable to take my eyes off her wandering hands as they make their way up her stomach, stopping at her tits and squeezing them in a way that makes my fists clench. We both take a sharp breath in as she bites her bottom lip once more, making me think she's enjoying this more than she's willing to admit. Carrying on her assent, she leisurely pushes her hair back, tips her head back, and rolls her hips as her hands start making their way back down. That's all it takes to break me. My willpower up and left the moment her hips moved. My fingers are sore and my knuckles white where I'm gripping the chair so hard, but I can't take it anymore, I'm done fighting this.

Reaching out, I grab a hold of her thighs, making her jump a little. Before she has a chance to object, I run my hands up and round to her ass. I want nothing more than to feel her pussy, but I need to play safe. Giving her cheeks a gentle squeeze, the sharp intake of breath, and the light pink hue in her cheeks let me know this is okay. So, I pull her closer, getting her exactly where I want her.

"Now now, Mr. Pierce, the rules are there for a reason." She teases, and I smile her a smile that quickly fades when I see the look in her eyes. She makes no effort to move my hands, so I give her ass another squeeze as I pull her down further, pushing her onto my cock. Knowing the moment she feels just how hard it is, when she lets out a little gasp and her pink hue is quickly replaced with a beautiful shade of red.

"Rules are made to be broken, doll." She opens her mouth to say something but before the words are out, I push forward and crash my lips to hers, taking advantage of the moment and thrusting my tongue inside. Her tongue immediately greets mine as she pushes her hands into my hair. Mimicking her actions as I move my hands up, I grab and pull her hair causing her to moan into my mouth. Then I pull again, being sure to thrust my hips, leaving nothing to the imagination and letting her know what I want. Her nails dig into my scalp as she breaks our kiss, letting her head fall back as she catches her breath. Needing my lips to be on her, I kiss her collarbone, grazing my teeth over her skin and then running my tongue up her throat. I feel her body tense when I sink my teeth into her neck, soothing her with kisses after. Melody makes pleasure and pain look good and I feel her body come alive as I selfishly take what I need. Lowering her head, her eyes lock with mine and the look of lust has my dick throbbing like never before. Considering how mad she was at me earlier I can't help but wonder what the hell has changed.

"Melody, have you been drinking?" I almost don't want to ask the question, fearing her response. But I know I would feel like a jerk if I didn't make sure she was okay. I know the boys paid for a dance, but I know she isn't being paid to do *this*.

"I'm sober enough to know what I'm doing but drunk enough not to care." That's all I needed to hear.

Surging forward, I grab the back of her neck and assault her lips once more with my own. Using my free hand, I undo her bra, sliding it off her body with her help. She grinds herself on my dick and I feel her wetness seeping through my jeans. It feels fucking amazing. Grabbing her ass with one hand as I start my descent down her body with the other. Making sure I grab her luscious tits on the way, but not spending too long on them as my desperation to be inside her is reaching breaking point. Rushing my way past her stomach, I place my hands on either side of her hips, pushing her skirt out my way. Grabbing hold of the flimsy material of her thong, I rip it off her. Her whole body jumps as the lace is whipped away from her most intimate area, leaving her fully exposed to me. Glancing down, I see the wet patch that she left, and I smile, knowing I have the same effect on her as she does on me. Kissing her again as I remove my jeans. She holds her own weight as I slide them down, not taking the time to remove them fully. Lowering myself back down, picturing exactly what I'm going to do to her but before I can, she grabs my dick. The shock has me stopping dead in my tracks, trying to focus on something that won't have me shooting my load in her hand. She rubs her thumb over my tip. Scooping up the pre-cum and places her thumb in her mouth. The sight of her, sucking it dry leaves me speechless, unable to think about what I should do next. She hums as she removes her thumb, smiling in pleasure as her hand makes its way back to my cock, stroking up and down as soon as she makes contact. My head falls onto the back of the chair in pure bliss as her hand brings me closer to the edge. She adjusts her body as she wriggles closer to me, kissing my neck while her hand grabs at my chest, the other releasing my dick and grabbing my hand, moving it towards her pussy. As I feel my index finger make contact at the side, I stick my thumb out and brush it through her folds, homing in on her clit. Before I can build up any proper momentum, she grabs my dick again but this time, she moves her body over it. She lowers herself onto me at a leisurely pace as I look up at her. The look of pleasure on her face takes my breath away and I realize I've been holding my breath when she's finally balls deep. I groan out in pleasure and she stops what she's doing and looks at me.

"Logan, I..." I lift my finger to her mouth, hushing her before she continues. This is not the time for questions, and I don't want her to overthink this. The moment she starts to think is the moment guilt and doubt take over her. And right here, right now Melody Grace is the only thing right in the world for me and I plan on enjoying her.

I quickly replace my finger with my mouth, running my tongue across her bottom lip when she opens up for me to delve in. Grabbing hold of her waist, I lift her up, slamming her back down and ripping the most beautiful sound from her throat. I lean myself back into the chair, so I can see her face as I do it again. I wanted to let her take control of everything' but seeing how she looks when she's sitting on my cock breaks me. I take any control she did have away from her as I guide her up and down, my attention shifting between her mesmerizing eyes and her exquisite tits. Seeing them bouncing up and down in front of me makes my balls tighten, letting me know I'm close. Moving my hand down, I zero in on her clit once again, there's no way in hell that I'm gonna let myself cum before she does. All it takes is two strokes with my thumb and I feel her pussy clench my dick in a vice-like grip. Melody throws her head back and screams out my name as her orgasm takes over her entire body. That's all it takes for me to finally shoot my load. This is the most intense orgasm I've ever had, and it feels like it's never gonna end. Melody goes limp and crashes down onto my chest as I ride out the last of my orgasm, with her head landing on my shoulder.

Feeling her skin against mine has me wrapping my arms around her, holding her tight as if my life depended on it, never wanting this moment to end. I know that soon enough, reality will come crashing down on us both but for now, I just want to enjoy this whilst I can.

NINETEEN

MELODY

Logan's arms engulf me as I collapse onto him. I need a minute before I venture back into the real world. That was truly unbelievable, I've never felt anything like that before. I haven't been with many men but I'm pretty sure that was not normal.

My hips start to ache, and I know it's time to get up and welcome reality back in. As I shift myself around, Logan squeezes me tighter, refusing to let me go.

"I don't want this to end yet, Melody. I'm not ready."

If I'm being honest, I wasn't ready either, but my body was telling me that I needed to move.

"I have to move, Logan, I'm starting to hurt." I slowly pull myself out of his arms and when our eyes meet, I see a sadness in them that I fear is reflected in my own. He leans forward and wraps his arms around me again as I start lifting myself up. I feel him falling out of me and the loss that I feel hits me hard. I'm sure he feels it too as he pulls back slightly to bring himself face to face with me once more. Tucking a stray piece of hair behind my ear, he cups my cheek. Leaning in, I take as much comfort from him as he will allow. Brushing his nose against mine, he gently places his lips against mine, giving me a soft kiss that says more than words could ever express. It doesn't take long before the easy pace is replaced with frantic need and desire. Wrapping my arms around his shoulders as his tongue slides into my mouth once again. Picking me up as he stands, he wraps my legs around his waist and makes no notion to move. Instead, he laughs, catching me off guard.

"I can't move, my jeans are still wrapped around my fucking knees." I can't hold back my laughter at how ridiculous this is. Unwrapping my legs, I slowly slide down his body. Placing my hands on his chest I risk taking a glance down. I've had him inside me twice now, but I've not had a proper look at his goods yet. My mouth drops open when I see that he is hard again but it's not just that. I'm not quite sure how I never figured this out earlier, especially as I had my hand wrapped around it, but he is huge. Like, so massive that I'm not sure how the hell that fit inside me.

"Like what you see, doll?" I'd love to have some witty comeback but I'm still in shock.

"It's just so big." I look up into his eyes as he starts to belly laugh, lifting me off my feet in a bear hug. Wrapping my arms around his neck, I realize how ridiculous I just sounded. Not wanting to embarrass myself anymore, I keep my mouth firmly shut. Logan places me back down and I take a step back as he pulls up his jeans, taking the opportunity to put my clothes back on. Guilt starts to creep in as I adjust my skirt. This was supposed to be the moment I walked away. Take back the control I seem to lose every time his skin touches mine. I always thought of myself as a strong woman, so why do I feel so weak in his presence? Tears sting the corner of my eyes as I start to feel sick. I need to get out of here before I do something else I'll regret.

Making my way toward the door, Logan grabs my arm as I reach out for the handle.

"Don't do this Melody. This is my guilt. You're not the one in the wrong here so let me carry the burden of what just happened. I won't pretend that I'm sorry, because I'm not, but I don't want you feeling bad about it so just stop it. Please." Looking up, I see the determination in his eyes. Now isn't the time to fight him over this but his words do nothing to ease the guilt I'm already carrying. How the fuck have I let this happen, again?

"Okay." That is all I can offer him as I look to the floor. He pulls me in for another hug and I relax into his embrace, hating myself a little bit more but allowing it anyway. Everything about this is wrong, so why does my body come alive any time I'm near him. Why do I feel like I have taken my first full breath every time he touches me?

His phone starts ringing, pulling us out of the moment. He steps away from me, taking it out of his pocket. Glancing down at the phone, he answers it with a frown. The look on his face worries me as he starts to pace, looking over to me every few steps. I can't make out what he's saying as he whispers down the line, but I see the tension take hold in his shoulders. It feels like an eternity until he gets off the phone, and his body language is screaming something's wrong. Even though he has his back to me, I can feel the anger flowing off him in waves. The sickness I feel now is different from a moment ago. I want to speak to him, to ask him if everything is okay, even if every bone in my body is screaming at me to leave.

"Logan?" turning around to face me, I can see it in his eyes. The upset and the worry,

"It's Gabby, she's been taken to hospital. I've gotta go." Before he has a chance to leave, I grab hold of his arm.

"I'm coming with you. Just give me two minutes to grab my

things." Seeing a million reasons to say no cross his face, he finally responds.

"Fine, I'll meet you in the parking lot. I just need to tell the boys I'm going." Logan turns and walks out before I answer. Not wanting to make him wait, I rush to the staff room to grab my bag and throw on some proper clothes. As I swing open the staff room door, I come face to face with Barry.

"What's up, Melody, is everything okay?" Seeing the tears in my eyes, he mistakes my concern for upset. "Did he hurt you? I swear to God Dee, if he laid a hand on you, I will go out there and shove that money where the sun doesn't fucking shine." Placing my hand on Barry's arm, I pull him in for a quick hug.

"It's okay, Barry, I'm good. Logan got a call that Gabriella has been taken to hospital, so I'm going with him. Is that okay?" He goes to respond, and a look of confusion crosses his face. He opens and closes his mouth a couple of times, so I cut him off,

"I'll explain more when I see you next, okay?" I think he can see in my eyes that now is not the time to talk about this, so he does the only thing he can do, pulling me in for a quick squeeze before leaving me to get dressed.

Making quick work of putting some clothes on, I rush out into the parking lot. Logan is waiting for me outside as a cab pulls up. Wasting no time, we both jump in.

The drive to the hospital was awkward, to say the least. We didn't speak at all after our initial conversation, but I glanced over to him every chance I got and the look in his eyes terrified me. knowing what we did only moments before he got that call, thinking about what we were up to whilst she needed him the most makes me feel guilt like never before. I can't carry this into the room with me when I see her, I need to get to the bottom of what the hell is going on with them and their relationship. And why the heck she's been taken to hospital. Avery said she looked awful the other day so it could be linked to that but whatever it is, I need to know before the guilt consumes me. I don't wanna take this to Gabby whilst she's not well. I'm so lost in my thoughts that we arrive at the hospital before I have a chance to ask any questions. The cab drops us off at the entrance and Logan pays before I can retrieve my wallet. He turns and heads in, not bothering to wait for me or even check if I'm behind him. I struggle to keep up with him as he makes his way inside. He navigates the hospital corridors like a pro, and this gets me thinking this isn't the first time that he's done this. Before I know it, we enter a sterile-looking room and Logan ushers me to a seat, indicating for me to sit down.

"Stay here until I come back, okay?" I open my mouth to respond but before the words come out, he turns and leaves. Leaving me with nothing but my thoughts to keep me company.

It was less than an hour ago that I had him inside of me, making me feel whole. Now I can't help but feel empty as he leaves me here to go and check on his wife.

What an awful person I really am.

TWENTY

MELODY

The hours pass by watching Logan pace up and down the waiting room. Every time I build up the courage to speak to him, to ask what's going on, he gets called away. Standing up, I decide enough is enough. I head towards the door I've seen various Doctors and Logan go in and out, I build up the courage to enter, but before I have the chance, Logan comes bursting through.

"Melody, where you going?" What I want to say right now is that I've had enough of this shit and I can't take much more. But what I end up saying is something more controlled.

"What's going on Logan? I feel like I'm going crazy sitting here. What's wrong with Gabriella?" Looking down at his feet, he makes his way back into the small waiting area, dragging me behind him. He takes a seat for the first time since we got here, then sighs and takes a deep breath, his face looking like he's having a hard time trying to find the words he needs.

"I can't tell you, doll. Not yet. It's not my story to tell."

Before I get the chance to reply, he is once again called away. But this time when he passes me, he grabs my hand and gives it a squeeze. A sad smile crosses his face. It's then that I see the war of emotions in his eyes.

Another hour passes by without a trace of Logan. With each passing minute, I get closer to thinking that I shouldn't be here. But every time I get up to leave, something holds me back. I need to know that Gabriella is okay. I have no right to this information considering what I've just done. The guilt has no place here right now, I can deal with that later. So, getting myself as comfortable as possible, I know I'm staying for as long as it takes.

Before I know it, I am woken up by Logan who is now sitting next to me.

"Melody, Gabby wants to see you, doll."

"What? Me? She knows I'm here? How? Why? Is she okay...?" Logan places his hand on my shoulder to calm me down.

"I told her where I was when I got the phone call, she was worried about Oz until I told her Avery has him. She was a bit confused at first, but I showed her the music video and gave her an edited version of how I know you both. I'll fill her in better another time. So, she asked if you were at work and when I told her you were, she asked if you came here with me."

Hours spent overthinking and worrying about what I'm going to say but nothing prepared for that. I didn't think about the fact that she might not know that I know Logan. Or how I'd explain it when I saw her. I was so wrapped up with worry and guilt, that it never crossed my mind. Taking a deep breath, I head in the direction that Logan pointed to, bracing myself for whatever is going to happen.

What I didn't brace for was how awful Gabriella was going to look. Trying to hide my shock, I rush towards her and hug her as if I haven't noticed. Her beautiful blonde hair has been replaced by a headscarf and her usually bright brown eyes look dull and sunken in, highlighting the bags underneath. She's much paler than usual and I feel how skinny she is as I wrap my arms around her.

"Hey Gabriella, how are you?" I wince at my stupid question.

"Honestly, not great. Can you sit down please Dee, I need to talk to you." She laughs as she responds, patting the bed and I don't know how to react. It feels like the walls are closing in as I take a seat next to her. The tension turns up a notch as I watch Gabriella go through a lifetime of emotions. She looks at me a few times, taking a deep breath every time but nothing comes out.

"There's no easy way to say this Dee, so I just need to say it as it is." Holding my breath, I wait for her to let rip, telling me that she knows what happened between me and her husband. Not wanting to look at her, I drop my head, looking at her hands instead. Placing her hand on mine, I'm still too cowardly to look her in the eyes as she takes the biggest breath yet.

"I'm dying." My head snaps up at the sharpness of her words, wondering if I heard her right. The words I think I heard don't make sense.

"I have terminal cancer. I got rushed in tonight because my heart rate slowed but it's okay now. Well, it's as okay as it is going to get." Everything slows down as I attempt to digest the words that came from Gabriella's mouth. She's dying? I find myself staring blankly at my friend. The words no longer make sense in my head as I throw them round and round, hoping that I've misunderstood, knowing full well that I haven't. Gabriella gives me the time I need to wrap my head around it, but I think all the time in the world won't help me understand or comprehend what she just said.

"Okay. we can find the best of the best, a great treatment plan for you, giving you a fighting chance of beating this thing. It's all good…"

"Melody, didn't you hear me. Its terminal. I've seen the best doctors, I have been on the best treatment plans, and it has all led me to this. There's nothing else that can be done. No more drugs, no more ways to delay the inevitable. I just want to live out my last days the best I can. Spend time with my son, show him just how much I love him and hope that it's enough to last him the rest of his life. Logan needs as much help as possible to prepare him for what's about to happen. He isn't ready for it, Dee. He isn't ready to be a single Dad but that's what is going to happen. But now that you know, you can help. Help him prepare for what is coming. You and Avery have meant the world to me this past year, I don't think I would be here now if it wasn't for you two. The support you gave me, without even realizing it, has been incredible. I'm sorry I didn't tell either of you, but I needed to have people in my life who didn't just feel sorry for me and you gave me that. I went to tell you so many times, but I chickened out, worrying that things would change. But you know what Dee? Life is too short for regrets, so please let us move on and make the most of the time I have left." The look of determination in her eyes has mine watering, but after what she just said, I refuse to let them fall. She needs my strength now.

"Just one thing though Gabriella. How the heck did you hide this from us?" A satisfied smile decorates her face.

"Good make-up and some fucking good wigs." We both

laugh despite the sadness that claws at my heart, but it gives me a moment's reprieve.

After another thirty minutes, I decide it's time to leave. It doesn't take a Ph.D. to know she needs some rest.

"Gabriella, I'm gonna go babe. I'll bring Ozzy in the morning like we agreed." She can only manage a nod as her heavy eyelids finally give in to the sleep she so desperately needs.

The fake smile I've had plastered on my face slips as soon as I leave the room. Calling myself a cab, I don't even bother to look for Logan as I make my way towards the exit. Outside, the world keeps on spinning as everyone carries on as normal. Taking a seat on a bench, I watch the people coming and going, wondering to myself if Gabriella will ever leave this place again.

The ride home is quick, and I haven't given a second thought about how I'm gonna break this to Avery. I stand at the front door for a moment, trying to gather my thoughts and think about the words I'm gonna use to tell her but nothing is coming to me. I enter the house in a daydream and manage to keep it together, until I look into Avery's eyes, and the damn I've built finally breaks.

The words spill out of my mouth quicker than she can process them. I know the look on her face, it was the same look I had not that long ago.

"How did we not know? How did she manage to hide it from us?" The questions come out the same way they did for me, but I'm too mentally and physically drained to give her the answers she wants.

"I need some sleep, Ree. I promised I'd take Ozzy to the hospital in a few hours, so I need to get my head down for a bit. Are you okay to keep hold of him until I can take him?" Avery huffs at me and I think she's about to refuse.

"Of course I will have him. I will also take him to the

hospital, so you don't have to worry about that." I start to refuse as she interrupts me,

"Don't you dare say no, Dee. We need to be there for her at all times now, 24/7, so you need to rest. You will be good for nothing if you burn yourself out." I know she's right but it's hard to worry about resting when you've just found out that your friend is about to die.

TWENTY-ONE

LOGAN

G etting out of that room, I needed a few minutes to make sense of the events this evening. When I'm with Melody all of the sadness of the past few years slips away enough for it not to be at the forefront of my mind. The coffee shop had not long opened as I wandered around the grounds, looking for some kind of distraction. Watching the hustle and bustle of people living their everyday life lets my mind wander to a place where the pain would never belong. Waiting for my coffee, I contemplate if I should get Melody one too. That's when it hits me, hard. I don't really know her. I've given her a part of myself that I don't share easily, yet I barely know a thing about her. When I'm with her, I struggle to remember my life without her in it. But at times like this, that's when it hits home that I don't know her at all. How does she take her coffee? I know she drinks coffee but is it her go-to drink, or does she prefer tea? What music does she listen to? I'd like to think that she falls asleep every night with me being the last thing she hears but the truth is, I don't know if she really likes my music.

Walking back to Gabby's room, I see Melody step out as I turn the corner. Not wanting her to see me, I step behind a door, but I keep my eyes firmly fixed in her direction. The smile on her face looks forced and my thoughts are confirmed as she closes the door. Tears fill her eyes, but she manages to compose herself before she takes her first step, placing her phone to her ear. I wonder for a moment if she's calling me but all thoughts of that disappear when I see her mouth moving. She walks past my little hiding place and doesn't see me as she turns the corner so I do what any reasonable man would do. I follow her. I follow her outside but keep my distance as she takes a seat on a bench. All those times I've played hide and seek with Ozzy come in handy now as I go somewhere I know she won't see me. I watch as she falls apart. Others don't see it yet, but I do. Her eyes tell me everything I need to know. The tears that are threatening to fall, causing a beautiful sparkle as the sun shines down on her. I watch her as all the different emotions cross her beautiful face. She's asking herself if there's something that can be done. Have we tried everything we can to get a different outcome to the one we're facing now?

What she won't know is that I have gone over and over the same questions for longer than I care to remember. She doesn't know that I have done everything in my power to get her the best treatment money can buy. Anything to stop my son from losing his mother.

The first tear falls and that's all it takes to get me back on my feet but before I reach her, a cab pulls up and she gets inside.

I watch as she tells the driver where she's going, and I know the best thing I could do right now is walk away. Forget about Melody and leave her to live her life without this mess dragging her down.

But I know I can't, I'll always be drawn to her. She's the light in the darkest part of my soul. Watching her leave without speaking to her nearly breaks me but she needs time. She needs to digest something that we've all been living with for years. She doesn't even notice me as the cab drives past, too lost in her thoughts to take anything else in.

My cell rings, pulling me out of my thoughts. Only one other person knows that Gabby is in hospital, so I know it's him without even looking.

"Hey Eddie…"

I update him with everything I know so far and although it didn't happen last night as planned, I truly see that I have to let the other guys in. For the first time since this started, I need to ignore Gabby and start letting the people who care about her the most know what's going on. We don't know how long she has left, and I want everyone to see her before it's too late. She might hate me for a minute, but she'll soon forgive me when she realizes how loved she is. Making my way back inside, I check my phone again to make sure Melody hasn't reached out. I want to be with her as she breaks. I want to be the one picking up the pieces of her heart and putting them back together. But right now, the best thing I can do is give her the time to adjust and accept everything she's learned tonight.

TWENTY-TWO

MELODY

W aking with a start, I reach for where my phone should be, only it isn't there. Where the hell did I leave that…? This isn't the time to lose my phone, what if Gabby or Logan need me. Rushing out of bed, I take myself to the kitchen where I'm greeted by the boys playing.

"Hi Dee dee. I missed you last night. Daddy called and ReeRee has your phone. He said Mommy's in hospital again and he sounded sad." Scooping Ozzy up, holding him tight in my arms I whisper in his ear.

"It's okay, big man. We're all here to help you, Mommy and Daddy now, okay?" He nods his head and throws his arms around my neck before wiggling free and running off to carry on playing with Zach. It takes everything in me to fight back the tears.

Just then, Avery comes in the back door and places my phone on the counter.

"Sorry, Zach heard your phone, so he went into your room to get it. He said he didn't want it to wake you." That kid had my heart from day one and things like this are why I never want it back.

"Is everything okay? Who was that?" Avery takes a deep breath and lets out a sigh. Even though I know it was Logan, I need to hear her say it.

"It was Logan. He was asking if we could keep hold of Ozzy for a while longer. He needs one of us to go over to the house and grab Gabby's bag. She forgot to take it when she went to stay with her parents, and it has some paperwork or something that she wants."

"Okay, I can do that, just give me ten minutes to get ready." Just as I'm about to turn and leave, I have a thought.

"One question, Ree, how are we meant to get into the house?" Avery smiles as she obviously asked the same question.

"He said there is a spare key in Ozzy's bag, and I have saved the alarm code onto your phone." Wasting no time, I whip my cell from the counter and get myself ready, making sure to hug Avery before rushing off.

On my way to their house, I try to call Logan, but he doesn't answer. I plan on telling Barry that I can't come into work for a bit as I will be helping them out, but that will have to wait. As I reach the front door, I am struck with a pang of guilt. Am I really the right person to be doing this? Obviously, I'm not but I know I haven't got time for self-pity. Letting myself in with the key from Ozzy's bag, I head straight to the alarm with code in hand, ready to punch it in. Only, it doesn't go off. Maybe they forgot to set it. Heading to where I was told the bag would be, I see a stack of cards and a box on the table. On closer inspection, it looks like some kind of memory box. A card for every age, right up to twenty-one. Various things are scattered around and in the box. Probably best to leave that for now so I carry on towards Gabriella's room to get her bag. As I walk past what I know to be the spare bedroom, I see movement. But before I can react, Logan steps out,

"Jesus Melody, are you trying to give me a heart attack?"

"I could say the same. I thought you were at the hospital, that's why I came here to get the bag for Gabriella." Hanging his head, Logan quietly says,

"I needed to get away for a minute. Needed a minute to think." The words ricochet around my mind and a wave of anger I have no right to have surfaces.

"You needed a minute? A minute to what, Logan? Your wife is in the hospital and none of us know how many minutes she has left, but it's all good as long as you manage to get some me time, right?" Turning away, I head towards Gabriella's room but before I make it, Logan grabs my arm, swinging me back around to face him.

"Do you think I don't already know that? You have known about this for all of five minutes, Melody. I have been dealing with this for years. Trust me when I say that it doesn't get any easier. Did you see the stuff on the table? That shit screwed me up more than anything. It made me realize that I have to tell my son his Mommy might not come home. How do you tell a seven-year-old that they might not ever see their Mommy again?" Tears appear in his eyes and that's when I see it, he's had a while to process this, yet it doesn't appear to be any easier for him. You could have as much or as little time as you need, but it still hits hard when reality comes crashing down.

I want to hate him. It would make everything easier if I did. I wouldn't feel the pain in my heart that I do right now, watching him reach breaking point. If I hated him, I wouldn't find myself wrapping him up in my arms, trying to ease his pain the only way I can. I want to be angry at him but that would do neither of us any good. He has enough of his own guilt to carry so I doubt giving him mine too will be worthwhile right now.

We stay like this for a few minutes whilst Logan pulls himself back together the best he can. He takes a step back and the sadness in his eyes hasn't gone, but he seems more composed now.

"I'm sorry Logan. I had no right to say that." He takes my hand in his and gives it a squeeze.

"You're right there, doll. You had *no* right to say that, but I know you're only looking out for Gabby, so I'll let it go this time." A simple smile and the tension eases. Not wanting to waste any more time, I turn and make my way to Gabriella's room, or should I say Gabriella and Logan's room, and grab her bag. Noticing a book on the nightstand, I grab that too, adding it to her belongings. Logan decided to go and wait outside so that he can get some air. On my way out, I look at the stuff on the table and decide to bag it all up. This is important to her, so we need to get it done.

For her, and for Ozzy.

Placing all of Gabby's stuff on the back seat, Logan makes his way over to me, taking my keys from my hand he gets into the driver's seat. Shrugging my shoulders, I head to the passenger side.

"Logan, I'm not going straight to the hospital, I need to go to the club and see Barry." Without acknowledging me, he fires up the engine and indicates for me to get in. I've never been a passenger in my car before, it feels weird.

"Did you hear me? I need to…"

"I don't want you working there anymore, Melody. You're better than that sleaze hole." I take a moment before replying to him. I know he's not in the right frame of mind at the moment, so I remind myself to be calm with my response.

"Logan, first of all, I love my job. What happened last night has never happened before, and it will definitely never happen again. Second, I don't have to answer to you, so would you kindly keep your opinion to yourself." He huffs as he makes the turn towards the club.

I'm in and out in no time at all. Telling Barry that I needed time off went easier than I thought. The money made last night has gone a long way to helping Barry out, so once I told him why he insisted that I have the time off on full pay. I tried to refuse but he wouldn't take no for an answer.

As I make my way back towards my car, I feel the tension radiating off Logan before I even get inside.

"This place looked bad enough at night but in the day it's damn right disgusting." He's trying to find fault and I can't argue as much as I'd like as the place doesn't look great in the harsh light of day.

"Well, you don't have to worry for now as I'm off for the foreseeable future." The tension in his shoulders eases off slightly and a sly smile lifts the side of his mouth.

"Good." Everything in me wants to tell him that I'm not giving up my job. This place means the world to me and I'm not willing to give it up. But I'll save that for another day. Now is the time to focus on Gabriella. As we pull away from the club, I get a message from Avery.

The boys have just crashed so I'll take Ozzy as soon as they're awake.

I tell Logan about the change of plan and he heads to the hospital instead.

We go straight to Gabriella's room as soon as we get to the hospital and I place her bags on a table.

"I hope you don't mind but I grabbed the box from the coffee table too. I'm here to help you with that if you need

130

me." A single tear rolls down her cheek as she takes it from the bag.

"Thank you, Dee, I appreciate this, so much. Did you look, Logan?" A simple nod of the head makes Gabriella hang her head, "You weren't supposed to see this yet. I'm sorry I never told you." Logan makes his way over to Gabriella and places his hand on hers.

"You don't have to apologize, Gab, I just wish you'd told me so that I could've helped you. You don't have to do this alone, ya know." Lifting her head with a smile, she pats his hand in return as tears fill her eyes. She manages to stop them from falling as he walks away, and she focuses her attention on me.

"Can you help me, Dee? There's still a few bits I need, and I'd really appreciate a woman's touch with them."

We sit for an hour or so as she talks me through everything she needs to do and wants to put in the memory box. Just as I'm putting everything away, Avery arrives with the boys. Ozzy runs to Logan and he picks him up, taking him over to his Mom. Seeing the three of them together makes my guilt skyrocket. How could I be so stupid? I stand and stare for a moment too long as I feel like someone is watching me. Sure enough, Avery's eyes are on me and I can't tell if she's angry or if she pities me. Maybe she feels just as guilty because she also knows what happened and she's having to lie to our friend as well. Composing myself, I finish putting everything away. My guilt eats away at me as each minute passes and I take the opportunity to leave as soon as it arrives.

"I'm gonna shoot off home since you all seem to have everything under control. I'll be back tomorrow but don't hesitate to call if you need anything, Gabriella." Logan stands as I head towards the door.

"Let me walk you to your car." Seeing the look in Avery's eyes confirms that is a bad idea.

"Thank you, Logan, but I'm good. Give me a call later if you need a lift home." The words come out without thought. He nods, but I know he won't call. I kiss Gabriella on the cheek and flee the room, unable to look Avery in the eyes.

As soon as I get home, I run myself a bath in the hope I can soak away some of my sins.

I must have fallen asleep as I'm woken by a knock at the door.

"Dee dee, can I come in?" I wonder for a moment if I'm dreaming but the temperature of the water helps me realize I'm not. It's unusual for Avery to knock so I instantly worry as I tell her to come in. Taking a seat on the toilet, she turns to face me,

"Dee, I'm worried about you. I see how you look at Logan. I've never seen that look in your eyes before and I'm concerned that this is too much for you. I know that look Melody and now is not the time for..."

"I don't know what you think you see Ree, but it isn't there. Thank you for your concern but I'm fine. What happened between me and Logan was a mistake, and it won't happen again." She goes to say something else, but I see her shut down. I hate lying to my best friend but there is no way I can tell her what happened at the strip club. And I fear that if she keeps on, I will let it slip.

Getting up from the toilet, she leaves me alone once more. She's the one person who knows me best in this world, and I know she's right. Try as I might, I can't keep up this lie I keep telling myself. I care for Logan more than I could ever say out loud and I'm angry at him for letting this happen. I will be there for Gabriella for as long as she needs me, but I know I need to avoid Logan as much as I can.

TWENTY-THREE

LOGAN

Time passes like a never-ending nightmare. It's been seven days, so far. I used to watch Groundhog Day and think how awesome it would be to get the chance to live the same day over and over. I couldn't have been more wrong. This is torture.

Making my way back to the hospital, I decide to pop in and see Ozzy first. This has nothing to do with the fact that he stayed with Melody last night. It also has nothing to do with the fact that although I've seen her every day since she found out, I haven't had a moment to talk to her, touch her, or even just breathe her in without it being noticed. I thought that when she found out, things would get easier because I would have someone to lean on. Someone to talk to without having to hide how I feel, but the truth is, I've never felt more alone. Also, seeing Ozzy is the best thing for me right now. He is the other reason that I manage to keep my sanity in this crazy time. As I pull up to the house, I see Melody's car is still here, but Avery's is missing. So at least I have a shot of talking to her alone. Zach answers the door before I finish knocking with an out of breath

Ozzy and Avery behind him. Ozzy comes running as soon as he sees me, and it feels so good to hold him. This boy is my life and I'm finding it more and more difficult to keep a brave face for him. But I carry on regardless, giving him as much of me as I can. Placing him down, Avery waves for me to follow her into the kitchen and I know she saw the disappointed look on my face when I saw her. Seeing my boy run off with a smile on his face lets me know it's the right thing, him staying here. Avery makes me a coffee but doesn't say a word whilst she's doing it. I can see the questions going around in her mind. The lecture that she likely wants to give me about what happened between me and Melody. Handing over the hot cup, she finally breaks her silence.

"Why?" Is all she says. One simple word with a multitude of meanings.

"Why what, Avery?" She hangs her head as she collects her thoughts.

"I'm not normally such a reserved person, Logan. But I'm trying not to lose it with you as you have enough going on." I'm glad to hear that, "Melody is my best friend. I've known her longer than I care to think about right now, but I've never seen her like this, Logan. I'd like to blame it on the fact that one of our friends is dying but we both know that's not it." Hearing someone else tell me Gabby is dying unsettles me. I've been dealing with this alone for so long that it's strange hearing the words out loud.

"I don't know what you want me to say, Avery." Shrugging my shoulders, giving her the only answer I can.

"I don't *want* you to say anything, Logan. I just want you to let go of the hold you have on her. Walk away now before you end up breaking my best friend's heart." The words hit me in the gut as I put down my coffee. She is more likely to break my heart than I am hers, so I don't know what to tell her.

"Where is Melody? Her car is still here so I thought…"

"You thought what Logan?" I hear the anger in her voice and all it does is build up my own.

"I thought she was here. I want to talk to her Avery, if that's okay with you?" The rage radiates off her as she finally erupts.

"No Logan. It's not okay with me if I'm honest. I knew you'd turn up if you thought she was here, that's why I told her to take my car. D'you know what's also not okay with me? Fucking another woman whilst your wife is dying. Playing with my best friend's emotions is also not okay with me. In fact, I think it's a pretty shitty thing to do. You need to start putting your wife first rather than worrying about getting your dick wet."

"You have no idea what goes on in my head or in my life."

"You're right, Logan, I don't. But what I do know, is that I'm the one who's gonna be left here, picking up the pieces when your sorry ass breaks my friend's heart." There are no more words to say so it's best I leave before this escalates any further.

"Let Ozzy know that I'll be back to pick him up a bit later. I'll see myself out."

"One last thing, Logan. You set Melody up last week, didn't you? You knew she'd come running to the house, so you used that to get her alone." Nothing I say will make this okay. Avery doesn't understand what it's like for me and Melody. I did set that up because I needed her to myself for a moment but I'm not wasting my time, defending myself to her anymore. Avery does not attempt to stop me or follow me as I leave. I didn't expect to hear those words from her today, they caught me off guard. So, the last thing anyone needs right now is me and Avery falling out when I don't say what she wants to hear.

The ride to the hospital was quick and it didn't give me nearly enough time to think about how I feel. But as I park, I put on my game face again, ready for my time with Gabby.

The first person I see when I get in the hospital is Melody, walking in the direction of Gabby's room. Running to catch up with her, I pull her through the nearest door, not giving her the opportunity to say no.

"What the fuck, Logan?"

"We need to sort this out Melody, I miss you…"

"No, we really don't Logan. We haven't got time for…"

"You can't keep denying what you feel when we are together. For the past three years I've woken up every morning, wondering if this is it. Is this the day I have been dreading the most? But for the first time since then, I've woken up thinking about you. I miss you. I need you, Melody."

"You don't need me, Logan. You need a distraction. You need a plaything to take your mind off things. I can't be that anymore. I should have never been it in the first place. This was a mistake…"

"You don't mean that doll. I know you feel it too." Looking into her eyes I do the only thing I know, the one thing that shows her what I'm trying to say. Pinning her against the door, I kiss her before she has a chance to pull away. Claiming her mouth as if my life depended on it because right now, that's exactly how it feels. Sliding my tongue into her mouth, I fight against the resistance I am initially greeted with. She puts up a good fight, but I get what I want in the end. She wraps her arms around my neck as I tease her with my tongue. Telling her with my mouth what I can't say with my words.

Feeling the pull of my hair, I know I'm winning, she can feel it too. No longer able to deny what is between us, I deepen the kiss, thrusting myself against her. Pulling back, she gasps for air and I use the opportunity to kiss her neck.

"Logan, we can't. We need to stop." Slamming my lips back to hers, I let her know that I'm not done yet.

"Logan. Stop." Air escapes my lungs as she pushes me away. This can't happen. Not now. Not when I was finally getting through to her. Grabbing her waist, I pull her against me once more,

"I want you, doll." But before my lips land on hers again, her hand connects with my cheek and the pain is instant.

"I said no, Logan. I can't do this." Tears fill her eyes as she pushes me out of the way, slamming the door behind her as she leaves me here alone. It takes me a few minutes to get my head on straight before I finally follow after her. Lost in a world of my own, I walk straight into Spencer.

"Jesus, Logan." His thick English accent brings me crashing back to reality. As I look across from Spencer, I see that he has Avery with him. She has a firm grip of Ozzy's hand and only let's go when he signals to come to me. I try to shoot her a smile, but she breezes past me without looking, heading into Gabby's room.

"Bloody Hell, that was cold dude. What have you ever done to her?" I knew Spencer would see it too, but I just play it off as if it was no big deal. Spencer has been here every other day since I told the guys. After the initial shock and anger at me not telling them they've been great. Eddie, who already knew, has dropped by every day, normally later at night after everyone else is done. Hunter and Cody don't really know how to react to it all, so they send Gabby whatever she needs. They took the time to listen to what foods she likes and what her favorite drink is since the chemo, and they send it to her daily. Gabby told me she feels guilty for not letting everyone in sooner but what's done is done. We can't change the past, so I told her to enjoy the here and now.

I take a minute to hold Ozzy tight, despite his wriggles to be free. He runs to his mother's room the second I release him, and I follow with Spencer behind me. The moment we enter the room, Avery is shooting daggers in my direction and you could cut the tension with a knife. Spencer keeps looking to me for answers, but I have none that I'm willing to share right now.

Melody tends to Gabby with a slight flush in her cheeks, avoiding my gaze.

The next twenty minutes go painfully slow as no one speaks,

SHARON CORREIA

except for Ozzy who is telling his Mommy about the great time
he had with Zach last night. Gabby's parents have been amazing
with having him but Avery steps in as often as possible so they
can have time to recharge. I've tried to get back every night to
get him, but he's been asleep by the time I get there.

Avery stands up suddenly and the sound of the chair scraping
on the floor makes everyone jump.

"I'm off to the shop." Holding her hand out to Ozzy, he
quickly takes hold as he jumps off the bed, "You can choose
yourself some candy and a magazine if you want little dude." He
nods his head, happy at the sound of candy. Spencer jumps up
too as I pull out my wallet.

"Let me get that Avery." She whips the money out of my
hand before I finish my sentence, hearing Spencer nervously
laugh as he walks by.

"I'll come with you, Ree. I could do with stretching my
legs." They're all gone in a flash, leaving me here with Gabby
and Melody. For the first time in my life, I'm at a loss for words.
I contemplate leaving myself, coming back when Melody isn't
here. Maybe then the tension I'm carrying will be lighter and I
can relax a little. Without provocation, Gabby starts laughing,
looking between me and Melody and I think for a moment I
missed the joke.

"Aren't you all supposed to be making me feel better? So far,
all I've felt is awkwardness and tension. If this is because of my
situation then I strongly suggest you all stop it. I'm going to die,
I've accepted it. I think it's about time you all did too." I visibly
see Melody's shoulders sag as the words leave Gabby's mouth
and she is up, holding her hand when she finishes talking.

"You're right Gabby. We will sort it. We are only like this
because we care." The nod of her head leaves me with the hope
that she believes that is all it is. Melody backs away, making an
excuse to leave. I can do nothing but watch her go as I know

138

Gabby will know something's wrong between us if I act on it. Seconds after the door closes, Gabby grabs at my arm.

"Whatever is going on between you and Melody, sort it out, Logan." I open my mouth to argue with her. To explain that nothing's wrong but she is the one person who knows me better than anyone. She's the mother of my child so I give her the respect she deserves, by not lying to her.

"I'll sort it, Gabby, I promise."

"I don't need details Logan, but I can feel your pain and I know it isn't all for me. You've had more than enough time to get your head around this, so get your head out of your ass and make things right." She places her hand in mine as I nod my acceptance of her words, crossing my heart with my fingers. I have to accept the situation I have put myself in and the promise I just made her. I may not know how I'm gonna do it yet but one way or the other, that promise will not be broken.

TWENTY-FOUR

MELODY

It's been three weeks now since I found out about Gabriella but the pain of seeing her doesn't get any easier. Me and Logan called a truce after the awkward encounter two weeks ago, promising to make everything as easy and peaceful for Gabriella as possible. So far, we've all managed to remain that way. We finished her memory box a few days ago but I still like to go in early and spend time with her for as long as I can before she falls asleep around mid-morning. I've been searching the internet, looking at various things we can do to keep her memory alive and so far, so good. The thought of leaving Ozzy breaks her every time but she always manages to recover quicker than me, telling me off for making her cry in front of whoever else is with us. We always hug after the tears have been shed, it's her way of letting me know it's okay.

Arriving at the hospital, I make my way to Gabby's room, but not before stopping off at the coffee shop to grab us both a coffee. The coffee they offer you in this place is horrid, so the least I can do is get Gabby to have one decent one a day.

As soon as I enter her room, I can feel her eyes burning holes in me. Looking around the room, I see that no one else is here yet,

"Hey Gabriella, am I the first to arrive today?" Placing her coffee down, I take a seat in the chair next to her bed.

"I told everyone to come in later, they all needed some time out. Being honest, I kinda needed the time out as well." Feeling instantly guilty, I start to get up,

"Oh god, I'm so sorry. I'll leave you to it…"

"Sit down, Dee. I need to talk to you and now is as good a time as any." My anxiety kicks up a level as I sit back down, preparing myself for whatever she is about to say. A million things flood my thoughts as she sits, contemplating what she is about to tell me. Maybe she's picked up on the tension that I feel whenever Logan is here? I've always tried to act the same but maybe I tried too hard. Or maybe it's the guilt. Guilt is a hard thing to hide when it is eating at your insides, telling you to be honest. I'm not built to lie and that alone weighs heavy on me. But how am I supposed to tell the truth when it could destroy whatever time Gabriella has left? I didn't know Logan was married the first time, but I have no excuse for what happened at the strip club. I knew everything I needed to know then, but I did it anyway. For the past year Gabriella has been one of my closest friends, although as I think about it, I can't help but feel upset that she never fully let us in. Maybe deep down, that's bothering me too. She always did seem to keep us at arm's length, and we always accepted it. But the truth is, we accepted it because we love her. She's one of the few people here who accepted me and Avery, no questions asked. Most people where we live avoided us, thinking we were a couple, but Gabriella didn't care. In fact, she didn't even ask us for a long time. That was until we got drunk one night and woke up with all three of us in her bed. She freaked out a little, thinking we had done the unthinkable. It goes against her faith to be with someone of the same sex but again, she has never judged anyone else's life choices. She is very much a live and let live person. We had a good chat that day, opening up about everything. I've never questioned that day until now. We opened up to her wholeheartedly and it makes me feel sad that she never opened up about herself. If she had told us sooner, we could've been helping her this whole time, instead of living our selfish lives. As the words cross my mind, I know this is exactly why she didn't tell us. She said it herself, she didn't want us to treat her any different. And we're back to the guilt again.

"I have to be blunt with you, Dee." Her words snap me out of my daze, "I'm dying, so I haven't got time to pussy foot around."

I feel sick in anticipation of what she's gonna say next. She knows, I'm sure of it.

"Gabby, I... I..."

"I'm not mad, Dee dee, but I see the way he looks at you. There was a time when I wished that just once he would look at me in the same way. He never loved me, Dee. I mean, he loved me as the mother of his child, but he never loved me for me." The first tear falls but I'm not sure if it's for me or her, "We got married because I got pregnant. He's always been a proud, responsible man Dee, and he knew I would be shunned by my church if I was to have a child out of wedlock. So, he did it for me. We were married within two weeks, and life changed in a way neither of us expected." She looks off into the distance as tears fill her eyes. I don't know what to say to make this any easier, but it doesn't matter as she continues saying what she needs to say.

"The first time I heard him say I love you, was the night our son was born. And it wasn't directed at me, it was all for Ozzy. Don't get me wrong, I love the way he loves our son. Logan would go to hell and back for his family and he would do anything for me, but you can't make somebody love you. He's been the best husband he could be but now is his time, Dee."

My tears fall freely as the words dry out on the tip of my tongue. There's no way she can be right about this. I've seen the way he looks at her. It isn't a look of pity, it's a look of regret. I assumed that he regretted the fact that he had met me, but maybe he regrets the fact that he never showed her just how much he loves her.

"But Gabriella, I know he loves you. I see the way he looks at *you.*" She places her hand on mine with an assertive look on her face.

"No Dee, that's a look of pity. A look of sorrow for the fact his son is losing his Mommy and there's nothing he can do about it. I've only ever seen the look of true love in his eyes twice now. The night our son was born and the other day, when he looked at you. *You* are what Logan needs to be happy, and that man deserves happiness, Dee. He deserves a love that isn't one of obligation, but one that comes straight from his heart."

Fighting with all I have I can't control the tears as they flood my cheeks.

"You're wrong, Gab…"

"No Dee, I'm not but it's okay. If there was any other woman who I could've picked for my husband to love, it would've always been you. You've been an amazing Mom to Zach, even though he's not your responsibility. I just hope you will do me the honor of doing the same for my son." It's safe to say that this isn't what I expected to hear today when I walked in here. Words fail me as my brain struggles to digest the words spoken by my friend.

"I don't know what to say." A tear falls as Gabriella laughs but it passes as quickly as it came, and she looks serious once more.

"All I will ask from you is don't let him forget me. Remind him every day just how much I loved him. Also, you need to remember that I love you as well Melody. You have been like a sister to me from the very first day we met, and I can't imagine

143

any other woman giving my son the love he needs after I am gone. My marriage to Logan was doomed from the start. He married me because I got pregnant, and he stuck with me because of what followed. I found out I had cancer in the early stages of pregnancy, we'd only been married two weeks, but I didn't start treatment till after Ozzy was born. I didn't want to put my baby's life at risk, so I held off. I thought I'd beat it, convinced us both that it was over, but I was wrong. When he thought I was strong enough he told me he had an appointment with a lawyer. The day before he filed the papers, I found out the cancer had come back fighting. I didn't tell him about the tests and appointments beforehand as I didn't want him to think I was trying to make him stay. When they said the words terminal, I asked him, in fact I begged him to stay. I didn't want Ozzy to have to deal with us splitting up as well as having to deal with losing me. He gave me his word that day that he would stick with us and he never let me down. Now is my time to make sure he gets what he deserves, Dee and that's you."

Now the tears are flowing freely from Gabby. I jump out of my chair and wrap her in my arms before she has the chance to object. Much to my surprise, I feel her arms embrace me right back. She refuses to let me go so I make myself more comfortable on the bed with her and offer her all the love I can.

She falls asleep peacefully in my arms and I don't have the heart to wake her, so I let her sleep as I soak up this amazing woman. I don't even want to imagine what she has been through with all of this. Knowing that you aren't gonna be around to watch your son grow is a pain I don't ever want to think about. A bang at the door pulls me out of my thoughts as one of the nurses comes crashing in with the drug trolley in hand.

"Hello ladies. Time to top you up Miss Gabby." She stirs in my arms at the intrusion.

"Hey, Deloris" We both say in unison as she stops next to the bed, looking through the chart. Knowing I shouldn't be on the bed, I shuffle my way off and start pacing the room, thinking over Gabriella's words again, fighting the tears as they sting my eyes.

"You can go now Dee. I'm gonna be flat out as soon as this hits my system anyway." I know she's right, she's good for nothing when the drugs kick in, but I don't want to leave. Looking at her, I can see the toll this conversation has had on her too, so I know it's best if I do leave. I feel emotionally wrung out so I know she must feel the same.

"Okay. I'll be back later. Do you need me to bring anything in for you?" Her eyes hang heavy as she fights sleep.

"No, it's okay. Logan is bringing some stuff in with him later." Hearing his name from her mouth is like a kick to the gut as the guilt comes back with vengeance. Gabby shoots me a warning look, whilst shaking her head ever so slightly. Although I know it's the right thing to do, leaving her feels hard today. I play her words over and over in my mind as I make the drive home. Does Logan know that she wanted to speak to me today? If he did, did he know why? What if he doesn't know. Should I be the one to tell him what she said? It's all too much to think over right now so I do the only thing I know how; I bury it deep down in the same place I keep my feelings for Logan.

TWENTY-FIVE

MELODY

The next ten days pass in a haze of hospital visits, sleep, and kids. Maybe with the odd chance to eat in between. Any time spent with Gabby feels easier since our talk, especially when Logan's been with us. I haven't found the time to talk to him about what Gabriella said but I think that is a blessing in disguise, I wouldn't know what to say even if I did talk to him. The words she said still aren't making sense in my head yet. I did speak to Avery though but that didn't go great. She is extremely mad with Logan for reasons she won't go into with me, but she is also still not happy with me. She felt I should have denied everything to Gabby, letting her go thinking that her husband loved only her. But once we talked it through, she knew denial would have been wrong.

We both spent a little time with Gabby this morning, but it wasn't long before she insisted on us leaving. Her decline in health has been faster than everyone had hoped but she still manages to put a smile on our faces every time we see her. Ozzy has been spending the majority of the time with her parents, who have been amazing through all of this. They have helped me to appreciate the time I had with Gabriella, rather than mourning the time I'm going to miss. Me and Avery are sad we're losing a friend, but they are losing a daughter and that gave us food for thought. That's a position I can't and don't ever want to imagine. Every day is a blessing and they have taught me to appreciate every moment.

Avery took herself off to bed around thirty minutes ago and I know I should too because I promised Gabriella an early morning visit again. She always seems more alert in the morning.

Just as I'm clearing up for the evening, there's a knock on the door. Being sure to look through the spyhole before I even entertain opening it, I see Logan on the other side. I can tell by the look on his face that he's here to tell us what we've all been dreading but it doesn't stop me as I rip it open. The words we both know he's about to say die on his tongue as tears fill his eyes. His mouth opens and closes a few times but still, nothing comes out. So, I take a step forward and wrap my arms around him. As he pulls away, his eyes land on mine and he takes a deep breath.

"I don't wanna be alone."

The words he utters are my undoing. Taking his hand, I lead him to my room, taking his coat off as soon as we enter. I hear Avery moving about so I excuse myself for a moment. I know Logan needs me right now, but I also have a duty to my friend. Knocking on Avery's door, I let myself in when she answers.

"Logan's here Ree. It's not good news." She leaps off her bed and throws her arms around me and I feel her silent tears soak through my top, "She's gone, Ree." I struggle to hold back my tears as we share this moment together.

"Go see Logan, Dee. He needs you more than I do right now." Looking into her eyes, I can see she's sincere, so I give her another squeeze before I leave her and make my way back to my room. Logan is in the same spot I left him, looking like he's lost a part of himself and I don't know what to do to help him. I've never had to console anyone before, not like this. Shaking myself out of my thoughts, I walk over to the bed, where he's sitting, and place my hand on his shoulder. His haunted eyes meet mine and he wastes no time pulling me forward and burying his head in my chest, wrapping his arms around me. His grip is firm as I wrap my arms around his head, letting him know I'm here for him. We stay like this for a long time before I have to pull away. My body aches from spending too much time standing in the same position, so I have a quick stretch and then crawl onto my bed. As I place my head on my pillow, he quickly follows suit, placing his head back on my chest wrapping his body around mine. Still, no words are exchanged as we fall into a restless sleep.

I wake up alone and wonder for a moment if last night was just a dream but the note on the mirror confirms it wasn't. Getting out of bed, I walk over to see what it says.

Didn't want to wake you.
I have to let Ozzy know.
Message you when I have chance.
Logan xo

It hurts to imagine what Logan's going through now, having to explain to that sweet little boy that he's never going to see his Mommy again is heartbreaking. The pain they will both be feeling brings tears to my eyes, which quickly turns into tears streaming down my cheeks. I jump in the shower and let it all out, crying into the pouring water before I face the day. The combination of music and water hides my sobs as I try to wash away the pain in my heart. Now's the time for me to be strong for everyone else.

Finally ready to face Avery, I make my way out of my room, into the kitchen. Making myself a coffee, I glance over at the bottle of Gabby's favorite wine that me and Avery promised we'd drink together when the time came. Even though it's only 10am, I've never been so tempted to drink this early before. It sure as hell won't do me any good but maybe it can help erase the hurt a little, one glass at a time. Avery comes into the kitchen and walks straight to the bottle of wine in question, picking it up.

"Zach is getting picked up at 4pm. As soon as he is gone, this bottle is ours, okay?" Nodding my head in agreement, I grab her cup to make her a coffee too.

"This will have to do for now." We clink our mugs together, with a shared feeling of sadness as we face the first day without our friend.

I don't hear from Logan all day, but I don't dwell on this too much as he's probably having one of the worst days of his life. Instead, at 4.01, as soon as the door closed on Zach and we said our goodbyes, we raised a glass, as promised to our friend.

Four hours and three bottles later, after a good cry, me and Avery celebrate the time we had with Gabriella, reminiscing about all the good times we shared with her. The wine is having the desired effect on me, helping me block out all the negative shit that's happened lately. Knowing that I'm close to my limit, I put down the half glass of wine that I've been nursing when I see a message notification on my phone.

Three words. That's all it takes to sober me up. Avery looks over my shoulder, seeing the message for herself.

"Go." Not wanting to leave my friend, I shake my head in protest to her words, even though my heart is telling me to go.

"You made a promise to Gabriella that you would be there for him when he needed you. Don't break it on the first day."

"But we made a promise to be together and drink her favorite wine. I can't break my promise to you Ree." Laughing at my words, she points at the three empty bottles on the table.

"We've done that, Dee. Now go and be there for him." Picking up her phone, she orders me an uber, not giving me a choice whether I go or not. I lean over and give her a hug before running off to grab my coat.

The uber arrives in no time at all, barely giving me time to splash my face. Sitting in the back seat, I open up the message again, letting him know I'm on my way. Keeping the message conversation open, I sit, looking over the three words that changed the course of my evening. Three simple words that made my heart speed up and meant more to me than I'd ever admit.

I need you.

TWENTY-SIX

MELODY

H is words play over in my mind as I knock on the door. What could he possibly need from me? Hearing the sound of Logan's raised voice has me opening the door and making my way inside. I find Logan in the kitchen, hand over the sink with blood all over the floor and cupboards.

"What the hell happened Logan?" Rushing over to him, I take his hand in mine and inspect the damage he's done.

"I dropped my glass and tried to clean it up, but I couldn't find the dustpan." I go to tell him where they would be but decide against it as I feel the tremor from his wounded hand. It looks like he picked up the broken glass by hand, hence the cuts. The smell of alcohol on his breath is strong and as I look in his eyes, I see how bloodshot they are.

"Logan, where's Ozzy?" A blank expression crosses his face as he looks around the kitchen.

"Ummm... With his Mee-maw and Paw-paw. He didn't want to stay with me. He decided he needed them, so who am I to stop him?!" The look of defeat on his face breaks my heart.

"Don't take it personally Logan. He's a kid who probably wants to be spoilt by his grandparents. You know he loves you." Logan shrugs his shoulders once more as I get on with cleaning up the mess he's made of his hand. As soon as I'm done, Logan sways off into the living area, so I get on cleaning up the mess he made in here. It takes longer than I thought it would and it gives me time to be grateful about Ozzy not being here. I don't think Logan would be this drunk if he was here, but grief does crazy things to people. The last thing that boy needs to see right now is his Dad in this way.

Just as I'm finishing up, I hear Logan talking to someone. Not wanting to interrupt him, but also wanting to check that everything is okay, I pop my head out, hoping to pick up on what's going on. No phone and no other person in sight, he is talking to himself. I can't make out the words, but his body language is getting angrier and angrier as he paces back and forth. He becomes decidedly manic as I approach, so I grab his shoulders, hoping it helps.

"Logan, what's wrong?" His eyes meet mine, but he doesn't see me.

"Flowers. Flowers. What flowers would she want? Coffin? Who knew there were so many coffins? It's just a fucking box to bury them in. I just don't fucking know anything anymore..." squeezing his shoulders, I let them go as I walk over to the bookcase, feeling his eyes on me as I move.

"Everything she wanted is in here." Pulling the book Gabriella told me about off the shelf, I hand it over to Logan. "She told me where to find it when the time came. She has everything arranged already, you just have to make the calls to confirm." Logan turns the book over in his hands as his eyes focus for the first time since I got here. Opening it up, taking in all the information that she already took the time to sort for him. Falling back onto the chair behind him, he scans through the pages, huffing and puffing with each page he turns. By the time he gets to the end, he's laughing,

"Who takes the time to plan their death?" he looks up at me, waiting for an answer I'm not sure I can give so I simply shrug my shoulders.

"Gabby, that's who. Even in death she was prepared." Hanging his head in sorrow I take a step towards him, placing my hand on his.

"Logan, she loved you and Ozzy so much. She wanted nothing more than to grow old with you, watching her son grow into the fine man we all know he will be. Planning this stuff nearly broke her." His head whips up at my words, looking like he has just been slapped in the face.

"You knew?" Realization flashes in his eyes as he looks at me. "You knew and you didn't say anything? Why didn't you tell me, doll? I could have helped too." The hits just keep on coming as his shoulders sag in defeat.

"Logan, she never wanted you to deal with this. She wanted you to live in the moment and have the best of her whilst she was still able to give it. We all knew this was coming but she didn't want you to think about it when she already knew what she wanted. Me and Avery helped out where we could so that you didn't have to." I hope he understands that we did this for him and Ozzy. They have enough to do now, we just wanted to help soften the blow as much as possible.

"I still can't believe she isn't here. What am I supposed to do now? How do I move on?" His voice falters a little as the words come out.

"One step at a time Logan. It's all you can do."

Logan eventually falls asleep on the sofa and I busy myself with tidying the house. I'm not ready to leave him yet and I don't plan on spending the night so I will just keep myself moving until the time to leave feels right. It feels weird being in Gabriella's house, knowing she isn't going to be here again, but I can't help myself as I work my way around, cleaning the mess of two boys who have never had to do it before. Not once did I come here and find a thing out of place, so the least I can do is make her happy by keeping the house in the same way she was used to for her and for Ozzy.

The bathroom was a disaster area that took over an hour to get as clean as I wanted, but Ozzy's room wasn't too bad. Just putting away toys mainly. I can't bring myself to enter Gabby's room, so I move on to the spare room, smelling everything that is Logan as soon as I open the door. The butterflies in my stomach hit hard as I cross over the threshold and I'm not sure if it's because of the smell, or the guilt of being in this room as he sleeps it off on the sofa.

It's probably for the best if I don't mess with too much. I don't want him to think I was snooping but I still tidy up a little, moving anything out of the way that he might trip over in his drunken state. The ensuite though, that is something I really can't leave. It looks like it hasn't been cleaned in months. It's not dirty, as such, it's just silly things like the shower door needs a good scrub and towels need picking up off the floor as they are starting to smell damp. That is where I start as I scoop up the towels, taking them to the washing machine to get them washed and dried before Logan even wakes. He is still sound asleep on the couch when I check on him, but I'm not surprised considering how much he has drunk. He'll probably be sleeping till gone midday. Watching him sleep brings me my own sense of comfort as I make my way back into his bathroom.

TWENTY-SEVEN

LOGAN

I sense Melody as she walks past me and makes her way towards the kitchen and for the first time in a long time, I wake with no pain in my heart. I appreciate this is hugely inappropriate considering I've only just lost my wife but there's something about her that calms me like never before. I have no idea how long I have been asleep or what she is up to, but I remain still, not wanting to disturb her and let her know I am, in fact, awake. My skin tingles as I feel her walk towards me once more, hesitating as she passes by. She's worried about me, I know, and the decent thing to do would be to let her know I'm okay. But the truth is, I'm not okay. I need her now more than ever. This is wrong in so many ways and I know she won't understand. If I'm honest, I don't understand myself, but I don't want to be without her right now. My mind is running wild as I lay here, letting time pass me by, listening to Melody in the distance.

I know it's time to get up when things go quiet. The alcohol lets me know it's still in my system as I rise to my feet and head in the direction the noise was just coming from. Standing in my bedroom doorway, I see her, sitting on the end of my bed. Her head is in her hands and her shoulders are hunched together, so I watch for a moment, to see if she's crying. Through everything that's happened, she's remained strong, and I haven't seen her break once. It's about time she let it out and it's about time I stepped up for *her*. Her head shoots up as I enter the room and she jumps to her feet as I step closer.

"Logan, I'm sorry I just..." Reaching out to her, I grab her shoulders.

"It's fine, you don't have to say a word. You look exhausted, please rest." I indicate in the direction of the bed and start to walk her over to the side.

"Logan, we can't..." The look in her eyes tells me that she thinks I want something else.

"No doll, that's not what I mean. Lie down, rest and we can talk. You need to let it all out, everything I can see you holding on to. Please, let me help you the way you're helping me. Let me be there for you too." Finally, she lets me turn her towards the bed, laying down as instructed. As I turn and make my way round to the other side, I notice all of the work she has done. My room was a mess when I left, I haven't had the time to worry about keeping it tidy with everything that has been going on but now, it's spotless. She must have spent all night cleaning. Shaking it off, for now, I get in bed next to her, face to face at last. I see the sorrow in her eyes as she looks at me but I'm not sure if it is meant for me or her own sorrow shining through.

"Tell me what you're thinking. Let me in." Noting the hesitation, I give her a minute before reaching out to grab her hand, hoping it brings her the same comfort that it gives me.

"I feel useless. I'm just trying to keep myself busy and feel useful for as long as I can. I can't take away yours or Ozzy's pain, but I just want to help you." Tears fill her eyes as she speaks openly to me and she has never looked more beautiful. I know in my heart this is the moment I should tell her that she doesn't need to try so hard, just being here for us is enough but I can't do it. The fear of her leaving me alone right now is too much for me to bear and I'm not ashamed to admit that to myself.

"You are helping more than you will ever know, thank you."

"You don't have to thank me, Logan. Knowing that I'm helping, even a little bit, is all the thanks I need." I panic, momentarily as she removes her hand from mine, but my worry is short-lived when she places it on my cheek with a sad smile.

"I'd be lost without you, doll. Promise me you won't leave, I need you."

"I'm not going anywhere Logan. I'm here for as long as you need me." She probably believes that the alcohol in my system will have me forgetting the promise she just made but she couldn't be more wrong. I will hold on to those words for as long as I need them. Most people would be ashamed of my behavior right now, but I can't help myself when I am around her. It's shameless. As she removes her hand from my face, I snake my arm under her shoulder and pull her close to me. I need to feel her next to me. To feel her skin on mine and to hear her heartbeat, strong and steady. Holding her this close calms my soul in a way I never thought possible and brings me a peace that I never knew existed. I always believed that being with a woman was nothing more than sexual chemistry but being here now, makes me question everything I thought I knew. Let me be clear though, the sexual chemistry between us is astronomical but it's in the moments like this that you truly discover how you feel about someone.

"Melody?" The quiver in my voice has her eyes meeting mine. "Can I kiss you?"

"Logan, I, I…" Her eyes drift from mine and I'm terrified I'm losing her. This is a moment where so deserves honesty from me. She needs to hear from me just how selfish I've been.

"I realized today that I've never asked you, I've always taken.

But from here on out, nothing will be done without your consent." Doubt flashes across her features. Quickly followed by confusion.

"Logan, I don't know what to say. I don't think this is a good…"

"Stop thinking Melody, just feel me. I need you. I need to feel your skin on mine. I need to feel close to you, to know you can feel me too. Please, let me kiss you. You are in full control here, doll, just say the word and I'll stop." I see the hesitation and doubt, clear as day but I also see the need in her, she feels it too. Lifting my hand, I use my index finger to lift her chin, noticing her biting her lip. So, I rub my thumb across her bottom lip, pulling it out of her teeth. Her eyes eventually meet mine again as she nods, letting me know it's okay. Finally allowing me the thing I've been waiting for, her approval. Placing my lips against hers is everything I needed it to be and more. Relief floods my system as I slide my tongue into her mouth, deepening the kiss. Passion takes over as she moans into my mouth, causing me to lose control for a moment. Grabbing her leg and wrapping it around my waist, I thrust once against her, inciting another moan of approval. I need her to know that she's the one in control right now. She's the one who has the power to shut this down if I'm pushing her too far. So, I grab her waist and roll, placing her on top of me. Her lips never once losing contact with mine as she takes over, grabbing my face and deepening the kiss further, as she grinds against my aching dick. Never did I think this would happen, but I'll be damned if I'll do anything to stop it now. Everything slows down as Melody sits up, robbing me of her mouth. I can't read her this time though, unsure if she is about to run or not. Her eyes don't leave mine as she reaches for her waistband, pulling up and removing her top. Her skin is flushed all over and her breaths come in heavy as she looks back down at me, biting that damn lip once again. Shifting slightly, I know exactly what I'm doing as I rub against her and her mouth drops open. Seeing her cheeks flush the deepest shade of red has me nearly shooting my load but I reign it in as I sit up and take her lip in between my teeth, biting down before catching her gasp in my mouth and swallowing it. The next few moments are frantic as we remove all our clothes, finally lying side by side as naked as God intended. For the first time in my life, I'm unsure what to do with myself. Not wanting to miss a moment of this time and take in everything as it happens. If I've learned one thing lately, it's that life is short and for living. This moment seems to go on forever, just me and Melody staring into each other's eyes, so I reach out, tucking a stray hair behind her ear and break the silence.

"You're in control here, doll. We can stop now and go to sleep if that's what you want?" I still can't figure out the look in her eyes as she shuffles to be closer to me. I open myself up to accept any form of contact she wants to give me and as I do, her lips connect with mine and nothing has ever tasted sweeter. I place my hand on her hip, but I don't pull her against me, even though I'm crying out to do just that. I really do want her to be the one in control. Her body finally connects with mine as she wraps her leg over my waist, pulling me towards her. The skin-on-skin contact with Melody feels amazing and this is a moment I bask in, being sure to memorize how this feels. How *I* feel. She pushes me onto my back and easily follows as she gets on top of me, taking everything she needs and more for the rest of the night.

TWENTY-EIGHT

MELODY

The day of the funeral arrives in the blink of an eye. Gabriella had everything planned and in place already so all we had to do was book it in with the undertaker, who happened to have a spot only six days after she had passed. Things between me and Logan have been... weird. We have spent every moment together, but we haven't been intimate since that night. He told me that the spare room has been his bedroom for a while now, but it still didn't feel like the right time to tell him anything that Gabriella shared with me. Ozzy has been staying between here and his Mee-maw's house and so far, he seems to be dealing with it all really well. The funny thing is, he hasn't asked once why I'm here, probably because he's used to my face. Logan has been distant for the most part. To be honest, he has been drinking every night and passing out rather than going to sleep. It's a painful process to watch but I know it's what he needs to get it out of his system. Eddie has been a bit of a Godsend for me, helping me to try and understand Logan's frame of mind but also being there for Logan when he needs a friend to speak to. I tried to be his friend at first, trying to prompt him to open up about things but it was not a good idea. We ended up arguing, with me packing a bag only to have Logan stop me before I made it out of the door. Cody has also been stopping by and if I am totally honest, he has been amazing. He is exactly what I needed right now, making me laugh in his silly, immature way. The stories that he and Hunter tell me are insane. Tales of their sexcapades that I swear come straight out of a book. The two of them together are the light relief we all need in this difficult time. Spencer has been a bit more distant, but he's still checked in every day so far, making sure we want for nothing. I can't decide if this is just who he is or if maybe it's hit him harder than anyone realizes. All of these things combined make me realize they're much more than just a band, they're a family. Avery has been in and out as much as she can too, taking Ozzy to the park with Zach and just generally helping out. I still get the impression she isn't happy with me right now but with everything and everyone around us, she hasn't voiced it yet. We should probably have a girl's night soon so that she can get it all out of her system, and also because I miss her. Since the day she got pregnant with Zach, I've barely left her side so this feels like a lifetime to us, to have been away from each other for this long.

I wanted to stay at home last night, so there was no risk of Gabriella's Mom catching me here, in her daughter's home but Logan begged me to stay. So how could I say no? Trying to get myself ready as quick as possible, so that Jenny doesn't have to see me walking out of Logan's bedroom, was a lot easier said than done. Logan ended up in a bit of a state as he looked for his shirt this morning, not happy with the one he had already chosen so I ended up spending time sorting this out and calming him down. It's crazy to think that I haven't known Logan that long, but he already leans on me way more than he should. I know it isn't all about the sex for him for obvious reasons but it's like he just needs human contact. The warmth of another person seems to help him at the moment and I'm happy to be the one he gets it from.

Sitting on the edge of the bed, I put on my shoes before sneaking out of here.

As I pass, I notice Gabriella's bedroom door open. Stopping to take a peek in, Jenny is sitting on her bed, looking unsurprisingly sad. She looks up and catches me watching her and gestures for me to come in. Taking a seat on the bed next to her, I notice she has a picture of a young Gabriella in her hands.

"She was such a happy little girl, always full of life. Did you know that I couldn't have any more children after Gabby?" Looking up at me, I don't know what to say as I struggle to push out the words.

"No one ever told me that, no."

"Oh, I don't suppose you would know as we never really speak about it. I had to have a c-section with Gabby and after they delivered her, they found a tumor. Times were different then, so they didn't think to put me back together before operating, they just went right in and ended up removing everything. My womb, my ovaries and even a small part of my cervix. That tumor took away any chance of me having more children but I'm not going to complain too much as I had my beautiful baby girl. They told me that if they hadn't caught it when they did, I would have been dead within a month and because I was already pregnant, that hid all of my symptoms. I've blamed myself every day since the day my Gabby got diagnosed. Maybe if I had noticed sooner then something could have been done." Wrapping my arm around her, I pull her in close.

"That wouldn't have made any difference Jenny and you know that. You need to stop punishing yourself for something that you could have never controlled." Wiping her tears as she pulls away, Jenny glances at the picture lovingly.

"I know dear, but I can't shift this uneasy feeling. She

deserved more." I can't argue with that, she did deserve more. Glancing at my watch, it isn't long now until our car will arrive, but I almost don't want to disturb Jenny whilst she is so consumed with her thoughts. Standing up to leave, I think it's best to give her a moment to herself but just as I get to the door, she calls me.

"Thank you for everything, Melody. We don't know what we would have done without you here."

"I would do anything for Gabriella and Ozzy, I love them like family."

"And Ozzy adores you too. Nearly as much as his Dad." The guilt that flushes my skin must be noticeable to Jenny as she looks at me and smiles. "Oh, don't be like that about it. Gabby told me everything before she left us. We all saw the way Logan was looking at you, so she thought it best for everyone that we knew."

"Jenny, I never meant to…"

"Melody, you don't have to explain anything to anyone, including me. Gabby told us what a beautiful soul you are, and I have to say, I don't disagree. Gabby and Logan loved each other very much but we all knew that they weren't in love. He did everything he thought he should. I mean, what man in today's day and age marries a woman he gets pregnant? All because of her faith? He did everything to make sure things were right for Gabby, even though we told them they didn't have to. He is a man who takes his responsibilities very seriously and will do whatever it takes to make things right. It's his time to love now Melody and I'm glad it's you."

Words escape me as I leave the room, trying to fight back the tears that are threatening to fall. That was the last thing I was expecting to hear when I got up this morning and it also made me realize how much I needed to hear that. The support and acceptance from Gabriella's Mom means more to me than I ever thought possible.

Gabriella's service was beautiful, it was everything I know she would've wanted it to be. She never had any plans for a wake but the one thing she did say was that she wanted everyone she loved to spend the day speaking fondly of her, remembering the good times, and accepting what's happened, exactly like she had. Logan decided it would be best to invite people back to his house, that way Ozzy can do whatever makes him happy. Jenny had been a great help with getting everything ready for people to arrive. It doesn't take long before the people who loved Gabriella come floating through the door, embracing each other whilst trying not to cry at their loss. And it takes even less time for the alcohol to flow. Before everyone is too inebriated, Jenny and Des take Ozzy home with them so they can leave everyone else to drink and celebrate Gabriella's life more freely. And celebrate we all did.

TWENTY-NINE

MELODY

The day went by exactly how I hoped it would. Celebrating Gabriella's life came easily to us all as she was very loved, and everyone tried their best to keep it as happy as possible for the sake of her son. Ozzy was obviously sad, but he smiled along with every story told of his Mom, remembering the good times we all shared.

Thankfully Logan took himself off to bed a while ago with his emotions all over the place.

Not long after, people started to go, leaving me to do clean up. When I make my way into the kitchen I jump out of my skin as I am greeted by a daydreaming Spencer.

"Jesus Spencer, are you trying to give me a heart attack?"

With a look that matches mine, Spencer replies.

"I could ask you the same." It doesn't take long for my heartbeat to return to normal but in that time, Spencer doesn't move.

"What you doing Spence? Are you okay?" He looks at me, with a thoughtful expression before he finally speaks.

"Yeah, I think so. Just never really been through anything like this before. That's the plus side of having a small family I guess, not many people to lose." I think this is the most open Spencer has been and I can't help but feel a little sad for him. "Anyway, let me help you tidy up after those dirty gits." This is the Spence I've come to know, stiff upper lip whilst we keep calm and carry on. British to the core this boy.

"Can I ask you something, Melody?"

"Of course, Spence. Ask away."

"Why do you stay with Logan?" Shocked at the directness of his question, I ready myself to go on the defense. "I don't mean that in a negative way. What I mean is, why do you tolerate him? I know things have been a bit crazy and I'm a hundred percent sure there are things between the two of you that only you know. But why do you tolerate him and the way he is right now?"

Despite all the chaos, I've thought about this a few times myself lately.

"Honestly Spence, I'm not sure. He's hurting at the moment so it's easier to let it go for now. I love his boy as if he were my own but that's because I've known him longer than I've known Logan. Ozzy is best friends with my best friend's son, and I've watched them grow. I never want to miss out on that, ever. Gabriella was my friend and I know this is what she wanted. She needed to know that her boys would be looked after in their time of need. It's the least I can do considering what I did." The shame takes over, forcing me to look at the floor as I fight back the tears.

"That's not your shame to carry, Melody. You didn't know about them. Also, Gabby told you she never held that against you, not once. She knew before the words ever left your lips and she never had to forgive you because, in her eyes, you never did anything wrong. Her and Logan were done, and she made her peace with that a long time ago. Long before you showed up."

Looking into Spencer's eyes I believe every word he's

saying. Gabby was dying when she told me it was okay, and I had to believe her because that's all I had. Spencer has nothing to gain by telling me this.

"How do you even know that Spence?"

Breaking eye contact with me, he turns and walks over to the kitchen counter, casually leaning against it before speaking.

"I spent a lot of time with Gabby at the end. Even before that really but we got closer in her final days. I've never lost anyone, as I said before and I was struggling to get my head round it. So, I did the only thing I knew how. I asked Gabby what I was supposed to do. How do I deal with losing someone I care about? She opened up to me in a way I never expected, and I will cherish my time with her, always."

Hearing the words coming from Spencer's mouth leaves me breathless.

"Wow, Spence, that was deep. You know I'm here if you ne…"

"Anyway, that's enough of that emotional shite. Let's get this place clean, shall we."

"You don't have to…"

"I insist. My mother told me to never leave a beautiful lady in distress."

Blushing at his words, we get on and clean up the mess everyone left behind.

Cleaning tends to be easier when there are two of you, and me and Spencer have this place ship-shape in no time at all.

It's just gone midnight by the time we finish, and the tiredness hits me hard. Trying but failing to hide a yawn that escapes without any proper warning.

"I can stay here if you need me to Dee?"

"No, it's okay. He will be sleeping it off for the rest of the night anyway."

Spencer picks my cell up off the table, grabbing my hand and placing my thumb on the sensor to unlock it. If I wasn't so tired,

I would probably have questions. Instead, I raise my eyebrow in the hope that he gets what I'm trying to communicate. Before he answers, his phone starts ringing in his pocket, but he makes no motion to answer it.

"I've just put my number in your phone, and I now have yours. Ring me if you need anything Dee."

The softness in his voice lets me know that he really means that. I've never taken the time to speak to Spencer before and I can honestly say I regret that now. You always think because these boys are rock stars that they know exactly what they want. You forget that they feel too. Everything isn't always sunshine and groupies. Sometimes there are bumps along the way.

"Thanks Spence. Not just for that, but for everything. Thank you for being there when I didn't realize I needed you." He holds out his arms for a hug and I waste no time taking him up on his offer. It feels warm and safe being in Spencer's arms and it was exactly what I needed after the emotional day. Sighing, I release him and step back, taking in his downtrodden features. Leaning towards him, I kiss him on the cheek as his eyes explore the floor. Finally, he lifts them to meet mine, giving me a small smile as he turns and heads towards the door. He stops just before he shuts it, turning to me.

"If he ever does anything to hurt you Dee, leave his ass. I'm only a phone call away and I will make sure you want for nothing." My mouth drops open at the unexpected words as he closes the door behind him, this very much seems to be the theme for today.

Shaking off Spencer's words which rattle around in my head, I grab the garbage bag we filled and head towards the kitchen, dropping it in shock before I make it. Logan is standing in front of me wearing nothing but stonewash jeans and a sinister look.

"Logan, you scared me. What are you doing standing there?"

He doesn't say a word as his eyes explore my body. Seeing him there, leaning against the doorframe so casually has my insides clenching. This man may be a mess right now but there is no mistaking that look in his eyes. The same look that has my panties wet without a damn word being spoken. Pushing off the doorframe, he stalks towards me, his eyes not leaving mine for a single moment.

"Logan..." He presses two fingers to my lips, stopping me from finishing. I stare at him for what seems like an eternity but still, he doesn't utter a word. Sliding his fingers down, pulling on my bottom lip as he goes, he hooks my chin forcefully tilting my head up as he takes another step closer. The tension in the air is thick as the heat from his body penetrates my own, causing me to shudder involuntarily. The cocky smirk that paints his face lets me know that he's got me exactly where he wants me. But before I take a deep breath, it's already gone and replaced with the serious face I'm used to, only this time there's something else. Something dark that I've never seen before. Still, no words leave Logan's mouth as he grabs my face, squeezing slightly as his lips smash against mine. There is nothing loving about this kiss. This is all passion. His tongue invades my mouth as if he owns it and the truth is, he probably does. The grip he has on me is borderline painful as his other hand grips my hip, pushing me up against the wall behind me, his lips briefly leaving mine as my back slams against it. He raises his lip in a snarl as he attacks my mouth once again.

Still no words.

He releases his grip on my jaw and his hands travel down my body, not stopping at all on his descent. Pushing my dress up and bunching it around my waist, he rips my panties from my body, not even taking the time to push them down. I feel a shot of cold air as he pulls his body away slightly, his lips never leaving mine, as he undoes his jeans. The warmth is quickly replaced as he grabs the back of my legs, lifting me up and wrapping my legs around him. Lining me up just right, he enters me hard and fast. Not stopping for a moment as he pulls back and pushes in again, breaking our kiss to let out a growl. Not once breaking rhythm as he slams into me over and over again. My nails dig into his shoulders as he pushes me closer to my release.

Suddenly, he stops. Trapping me to the wall with his body. Releasing my legs, he grabs my arms, lifting them and pinning them above my head with one hand as the other lands firmly on my ass giving it a squeeze. Not even taking a moment to catch a breath, he slams into me again as his lips attack mine once more, bringing me closer to the edge. All the air escapes from my lungs and I try to pull back a little, realizing for the first time that I'm trapped. Fear is what I should feel right now but the thought of being trapped by this man excites me more than I would ever admit. Logan senses my shock and breaks the kiss but not stopping as his lips run across my jaw, nipping as they go. He sinks his teeth into my neck and that's all it takes to have me falling over the edge I've been teetering on. My orgasm hits hard as a scream rips from my throat, unable to hold it down anymore. I hear him growl at his own release as the thrusts finally slow down.

Still without a word.

I don't know where to look as I feel his eyes on me. He makes no attempt to pull out, but he does release my wrists. My hands land on his shoulders and that's when I see the marks he left behind. My wrists glow red, and I hate to think what the rest of me looks like. Finally, I lift my eyes to meet his and for the first time in a while. Logan looks... Happy. I smile as I raise my hand to cup his cheek, still unsure what to say. Wrapping his hand around my back, Logan pulls me away from the wall and carries me into his bathroom, managing to stay inside me the whole time. Placing me down on the vanity edge, he finally pulls himself free and the loss is instant. Taking a washcloth, he wets it under the hot tap and proceeds to clean me up. I wouldn't normally let this happen, but I don't want to interrupt him as in this moment, he finally seems okay. Once he's happy with the job he's done, he stands me up and turns me to face the mirror. Stepping in close behind me, he grabs me under the chin again, making sure I see what he wants me to.

"You see that doll?" I nod my head as much as I can within his grip, and he moves his mouth closer to my ear as he continues.

"Everything you see right now, is mine." Turning my head, he shows me the bruise that is already starting to form on my neck.

"Mine."

Cupping my breast over my dress, squeezing as he talks.

"Mine."

Moving his hand down to my pussy, cupping and squeezing as he hums in my ear.

"Fucking mine."

And as the words leave his lips, his finger circles my clit, taking another orgasm with it.

My body unable to deny how his possessiveness gets me off in a way I could have never thought possible.

Another Guilty Pleasure of mine to add to the ever growing list.

THIRTY

LOGAN

Seeing Melody's reflection in the mirror as she reaches her climax again with nothing more than my words and a touch of her clit lets me know she wanted this. I thought for a minute that I'd gone too far, taking exactly what I wanted from her without saying a word. I was rough with her, really rough, but she got off on it as much as I did. But still, I spent the next two hours making it up to her, showing her the love I'm capable of giving, and by Christ that was just as beautiful. Seeing her fall apart as I whispered sweet nothings into her ear, and her pussy, gave me the life I didn't know I was missing.

I'd heard what Spencer said to her and it pissed me off. I needed to make sure that she knew exactly who she belonged to. Who was the only man responsible for her pleasure, and her pain from now on. Feeling her turn towards me on the bed snaps me out of my daydream.

"Hey, you okay there, Mr. Pierce?"

If I hadn't fucked her three times already, I would be inside her again now. Hearing her call me that does something to me.

"Why'd you ask, doll?"

"You look deep in thought. Just wanted to check you're okay, that's all." She probably thinks I'm thinking about the last twenty-four hours we've had and the fact I just buried my wife. I mean, that's what most people in my position would probably be thinking about, but she doesn't understand the agreement me and Gabby had. I'd rather spend my time thinking about being inside her. That seems to be the only place where I find any peace. Never having to think, just let instinct take over with her. It's funny how well I know her body considering I haven't known her that long. The way her eyes glaze over when you touch her in just the right spot, or the way she bites on her bottom lip right before her orgasm takes her. As I lie here, looking at Melody, I realize that I've never noticed any of this sort of shit with anyone else before. I was too busy chasing my own release. Does that make me heartless? Probably. Right now, I don't care enough to give it any more thought. Jumping out of bed, I head towards the door.

"Where you going, Logan?"

"I'll be back in a minute, doll. Just getting a drink." The smile on her face is beautiful. A look of contentment that you only have when you're truly happy. Well, you know what they say, ignorance is bliss. If she knew I was getting a drink of Jack, I'm pretty sure she wouldn't look so happy. Five minutes and a quarter of a bottle later, I head back to the bedroom. This should help me sleep a bit easier tonight. Standing at the side of the bed, I take a long look at Melody as she sleeps. The bruises that are starting to appear on her should make me feel bad but there's something beautiful about them. The one on her neck is especially beautiful because it's gonna let everyone know that she belongs to me. All the makeup in the world ain't gonna cover that up. I think my favorite one though, is the one on the inside of her thigh. No one else will ever see it but it gets me hard just thinking about it. Watching her come apart as I sank my teeth in

173

is a memory I will cherish forever. Being with her has unleashed a side of me that I never knew existed and I'd be lying if I said I didn't like it. I've spent my whole adult life doing what's right for others. This is the first time I've stopped and done what *I've* wanted to do and I fucking love it.

Just as I'm getting under the sheets, Melody stirs, opening her eyes as I place my head down.

"Hey, you were gone a while. You okay?"

"Why do you always ask if I'm okay? Unless I say any different, I'm good. Alright."

Sitting up slightly, she looks almost scared to respond.

"Okay. Sorry Logan, I didn't mean to upset you."

"You didn't upset me doll." I gently stroke her cheek before continuing. "Spencer is a different story though. I think me and him will be having words next time I see him." I see the look of confusion on her face, and she takes a moment to reply as I lie down and make myself comfortable.

"What are you talking about Logan?"

"I heard him. I heard what he said to you as he left. I heard him telling you to leave me and that he'll make sure he looks after you right." She sits upright, holding the sheet over her chest, depriving me of the view.

"That's not what he said Logan. He's just looking out for me, that's all." Turning away from me, she lies back down. Every fiber inside me wants to fight but I haven't got the energy for this now. The buzz of the alcohol has finally kicked in and I've gone back to feeling like I'm not that bothered anymore. Grabbing Melody's shoulder, I pull her towards me, lifting her arm and nuzzling into her neck before she has a chance to protest.

"Okay doll, you're right. Maybe I heard it wrong." I know I didn't, but I'll come back to this another day. Sleep is very much on the agenda now. I feel the words she is speaking but I don't hear anything as I fall into a deep, blissful sleep.

THIRTY-ONE

MELODY

W aking up wrapped in Logan's arms is something I don't think I could ever get used to. He isn't the most affectionate when he's awake but when he sleeps, he doesn't let me go. This makes getting out of bed damn near impossible without waking him, but I still somehow manage it. The ache between my legs doesn't go unnoticed as I make my way into the bathroom. *I feel this first wee of the day may sting a bit.* Breezing past the mirror, I catch the first glimpse of the hot mess I look like this morning, but I decide not to stop and stare. I can assess the damage after a nice, hot shower. Pushing the door closed, so I don't disturb Logan, I hop into the shower and wash away the sins of last night. Well, most of them anyway. Standing in front of the mirror with my hair still dripping, wearing nothing but a towel, I'm finally faced with the reality of how rough Logan was last night. Three fresh bruises line my breasts and as I run my hand over them, I feel them swelling.

But that's not the worst of it. The mark on my neck looks horrific, even this soon after. It doesn't hurt but I hate to think what people will say if they see it. The best thing is and the thing I'm struggling to get my head around the most, is the fact that I loved it. I loved feeling Logan's teeth sink into my skin and the pain which helped to heighten my pleasure. I don't think I have ever orgasmed so intensely in my life, especially when he bit inside my thigh. Lost in my thoughts, I nearly jump out of my skin when I look back up and see Logan behind me in the mirror.

"Holy shit Logan. What are you doing in here?" Shuffling my towel up, I try to hide some of the bruises before turning round to face him.

"Did I do all that?" The look on his face lets me know he already knows the answer to his question. "It looks so bad in this light." He takes a step forward and lowers my towel a little, looking over the marks across my chest. He gently strokes his fingers over the bruises, and I judder at the feel of his fingers on my skin. The concern in his eyes lets me know that he didn't intend to hurt me which I'm glad about because deep down, I loved it.

"Yeah, but it's ok…"

"Is it?" Two tiny words that have a massive impact on me. Is it okay? It looks horrific when you just look at the bruises but *is it* wrong that I love how they got there? I look to him for answers that I'm not willing to say out loud right now.

"I… I…" I have nothing.

"I'm sorry." The words bounce around the small space we are in and while I do appreciate the apology, I also feel like it isn't needed. He opens his arms and I step into them without a second thought. He grips me tight, but he loosens it in a heartbeat as if I will break if he squeezes too hard.

"Logan, you don't need to apologize to me, we're both consenting adults and…"

"I shouldn't have been so rough with you." Logan releases me and takes a step back, giving me another once over with his eyes.

"I'm okay Logan, I promise." He gives me a sad smile as he leaves the bathroom, leaving me to look in the mirror at the reminders of last night. I can't help but feel that each bruise is a beautiful story of the passion we shared. I've never felt this way with anyone before so the fact that I can look at these marks and feel nothing but joy is strange.

I may enjoy looking at them, but I don't think others would see it the same way. So, I apply makeup to the one on my neck in the hope I can cover it enough. Picking out an outfit is a bit more difficult as I only have a select amount here. Finding something to cover my chest is more difficult than I first thought. Turns out I like to show them off, who knew. I need to go and see Barry today as I need to get back into some kind of routine. I've loved my time with Logan and Ozzy, but I need to start getting back to normal. It won't be long before Logan won't want me around him and his son, so I need to get ahead of it and get my life back on track. I miss Avery and Zach as well, so the sooner I get everything in order, the sooner I can get back to what I know.

As soon as I'm dressed, I throw my hair up out of my way and head into the kitchen, where I find Logan.

"Hey doll, I've made you a coffee. You look nice, going somewhere?" Taking the coffee from his hands, I take a gulp and appreciate the rich taste as it coats my throat, sighing in appreciation.

"Yeah, I'm off to see Barry about picking up some shifts." The tension that rolls off Logan is instant, but I don't have the time or patience to deal with him right now. What I really need is to get back to reality. However much I want to be here for Logan and Zach, I also need to pay my bills. Placing my drink down, I give Logan a swift kiss on the cheek before grabbing my keys and purse and heading out.

As I enter the bar, I see Barry with that Biker guy again. Not caring right now if I disturb them, I pull up a stool next to him and look at Barry, trying to convey my concern.

"Hey Miss Melody Grace, how are you babe? Haven't seen you for a while. How's Logan and Ozzy?" Feeling biker dude's eyes on me I just carry on as if I haven't noticed.

"Logan and Oz are doing okay, thank you. I need to get back to work Barry, so when can I come back." The grunt that comes from Biker boy has me turning to face him.

"Barry asked if *you* were okay too, darlin'. But judging by the state of you, I'd say not." Shifting uncomfortably in my seat, I obviously didn't do as good a job as I thought covering up the bruising.

"I'm good, thanks for asking, Barry." Something about this man is irritating me now so I turn to face my boss again, but biker boy isn't done.

"Just say the word, darlin' and I'll have 'em good as dead by mornin'. Will even get rid of the body if you ask nicely." The smirk on his face as he raises his drink to his lips leaves me concerned. To anyone listening this could be mistaken for a joke, but I can tell by his body language and the look on his face that he's not joking. The look on Barry's face doesn't help either, although it probably mirrors my own.

"You can come back as soon as you want Dee, as long as you're sure you're ready."

"I'm ready, Barry. I need some normality back." Jumping down from my seat, I run out the back to put my name on the roster before Barry, or biker boy makes me change my mind.

Heading back into the bar I stop in front of the biker, whose name I can't remember.

"So, whatever your name is, what's your deal then?" Barry looks horrified at my line of questioning.

"The name's Troj, but I can have you calling me God by the end of the night." I feel my whole face flush. This guy may be a bit arrogant, but no one could ever say that he isn't gorgeous. "And my *deal* is to try and help Barry become a very wealthy man. Now, I'm not trying to be rude, darlin' but I've gotta shoot.

Places to go, women to do." His eyes scan down my body in a way that makes me go a bit weak at the knees. "Nice to see you again Melody. Barry, tell Avery I'll be back later if you see her." Barry responds like some kind of nodding dog as Troj turns to walk away, but the mention of my best friend sets me on edge.

"Avery? How do you know Avery? I hope she isn't just one of these women that you have to do?" Stopping in his tracks, he turns back around and walks up to me.

"You're Dee dee? I don't know how I didn't figure this out earlier." Laughing, he leans over to the bar to grab a napkin and pen. "You didn't answer my question, darlin'. So, here's my number, if whoever did this to you tries pullin' that shit again, you call me. Avery is just a friend, nothing more, but I like her, and I know how much she loves you. You need anything, you call." He leans in and kisses me on the cheek before walking out as if nothing happened.

"Well, that was weird." Barry's words break the silence in the room.

"Barry, what are you doing, doing business with these types of people?"

"Dee, I'm not gonna go into it now but you have to trust me. I know exactly what I'm doing, and I also know exactly what type of people they are." Everything inside me wants to push this with Barry but I just don't have the energy to fight right now. So, I nod my head, but we both know this conversation is far from over.

THIRTY-TWO

LOGAN

The days all roll into one, starting with a foggy head and finishing with one too. I don't even know how much time has passed but what I do know is that Melody hasn't left my side. Well, she tried to but we both agreed that wasn't gonna happen again any time soon.

I know Melody is craving for things to go back to normal, but I can't let go of her yet. A few weeks ago, she tried to go back to work but the evenings are when I struggle the most to be on my own. So, I decided to go to the strip club to see her. That's all it was, I wanted to see her, and be able to watch her as she works. Everything I care for ends up getting taken away from me and I'm not ready to let her go, so I kept an eye on what's mine. Trouble is, so did every other red-blooded man in that place. I felt the rage building more and more with each set of eyes that landed on her. Nearly went flying out of my chair when some guy lifted his arm out to touch her, but my girl is smart. She dodged him like a pro. Trouble was, I could feel eyes on me all night and I was starting to think I was going crazy. That was up until the last time Melody came over to me at the end of the bar, to check on me. That was when I decided to let everyone know who she belonged to. Turning in my chair to face her, I grabbed hold of her, pulling her in between my legs, and kissed her as if my life depended on it. The next thing I know, my girl is being ripped out of my arms and some biker guy punches me in the face. Melody's screams bring me back to reality and the words I hear being thrown around make me feel sick.

"Troj, I told you already. He isn't abusing me."

"That's not what it looked like from where I was sittin' darlin'."

Troj? She knows this guy? Getting to my feet, I absorb the words he spits at me,

"I ever see you manhandling a woman like that again, the next one will be more than just a warning shot, you get me?"

I don't really remember much after that, other than the fact this dude thought I was abusing her because of the bruises. She didn't appreciate it when I asked her to tell him why she really had them. She appreciated it even less when she confessed to him how much she loved it. Needless to say, she hasn't been back to Cherry Pickers since. I could pretend to be sad about it. But the truth is, I'm not. I hated her working in a place like that anyway.

Ozzy is spending another weekend with Jen and Des' and it is up to me to pack his bag. Melody had to go out and run some errands for Avery, leaving me in charge of this one. Oz helped me out as much as he could before he left for school but he's a kid, all he cares about is what toy he takes with him. Let's hope his grandparents have spare shit if it's needed as I haven't got a clue what to pack. Sitting in the living room, I resist the urge to have a drink as I know Ozzy will be back from school any minute now. Eddie said that he'd pick him up today as he wanted to take him out for a burger before he goes off for the weekend. Eddie has been here every day for the past month or so and I know seeing me drinking is killing him. But yet he still turns up, hoping today will be the day I say no more. I haven't got a problem, I could easily not have a drink if I didn't want to but that's the problem, I never don't want to. I'm not ready yet and I just want to feel numb, shut the world out for a little bit longer.

"Daddy." Ozzy comes bursting through the door just as I get on the slippery slope of self-pity.

"Hey buddy, did you have a good time with Uncle Eddie?" The big nod and huge smile on his face say more than words ever could. Jumping on my lap, he gives me a big hug and at this moment, I know this is what I'm living for. All the money in the world could never buy this feeling of unconditional love and acceptance.

"Mee-maw is here Daddy." And just like that, he's gone again. Grabbing his bag as he runs out the door with Jen.

Eddie follows me into the kitchen as I reach into the cupboard, grabbing a new bottle of Jack. "Thought you might wanna save the hard stuff for later at least, Logan?"

"Well, you know what they say, there's no time like the present." Ripping the lid off, I don't even bother with the glass, tipping the amber liquid straight down my throat straight from the bottle. I see the disappointment in Eddie's eyes as I finally reach for a glass. As always, I offer one to Eddie but unsurprisingly, he refuses. His battle was with drugs, Heroin mainly, but he decided it was probably best to give up everything, save any temptation.

"We need to talk about this shit with the paparazzi Logan. They are tearing Melody apart. Ever since they got that pic of you walking out of Cherry Pickers, they've been brandishing her as some kind of whore. It's not fair on her Logan and you are the only one who can do something about it." I hear the words Eddie is saying but I don't know what to do about it.

"What's the point in fighting against them, Eddie? They only print what people want to see. Who cares if they think that. We know the truth, isn't that the most important thing?" The paparazzi have always been a pain in the ass, and I've never corrected them before, so why bother now.

"You'd think so, wouldn't you? Spencer is raging about how they're treating her. He's angry at you for letting them say these hurtful things about her." Hearing Eddie say Spencer's name when referencing Melody makes me angry.

"What the fuck has it got to do with him?" I spit the words at Eddie, a little more aggressively than I intended.

"I don't know, Logan, but what I do know is he's hurting. Watching Gabby die changed him. It's cast a dark shadow over him that he is struggling to get out of." Shrugging my shoulders, I make my way back into the living room. I can't be dealing with this shit right now, so I shut it down for another day.

"What right has he got to struggle? It wasn't the mother of his kid that died, was it?" Knowing Eddie won't want to reply to that, I flick on the TV.

Before long, Melody is back, with bags full of groceries but before I can get up to help her, Eddie is there taking bags from her and going into the kitchen to unpack. A good twenty minutes' pass with them two in the kitchen but my guilt over this paparazzi business has me fixed to my chair, guilt winning out on this occasion. My pity party is interrupted as Eddie shouts bye, before shutting the door behind him. I know he's mad at me but he's just gonna have to suck it up and deal with it, I have enough to cope with without worrying about how I'm pissing everyone off in the band.

Heading into the kitchen, I walk up behind Melody, taking the opportunity to grab her and pull her close whilst she's so deep in thought.

"Jesus, Logan." Pulling away from me as quickly as I grabbed her, she busies herself with cleaning the kitchen counter. Before I let the guilt consume me, I grab her again, spinning her around so she is finally face to face with me. Taking her lips with my own, I attempt once more to ease the guilt and get lost in her instead.

THIRTY-THREE

MELODY

The smell of whisky on his breath turns my stomach and I try to think as fast as I can for any excuse to stop this happening right now.

"Milk. We need milk. Ummm, I better go and get some now before it gets too late." I don't give him a chance to reply as I slip out of his grip, grabbing my keys and purse. Heading out of the door quicker than I ever have before.

An hour passes yet I still haven't stopped anywhere to get any milk. Truth is, we don't really need any as Ozzy is with his grandparents and we barely use any when he isn't here, but I just needed to get away for a bit, not ready for our daily routine just yet.

It's the same thing every night. We have sex, he tells me he needs me. Depending on how drunk he is, he might even tell me he loves me.

Yeah, that came as a shock the first time he did it. I soon learned that it very much depended on what he had been drinking. The lack of acknowledgment the next day is what hurts the most. Well, the first time anyway. I know he cares about me. He shows me the best way he knows how. I think losing Gabby has affected him more than he cares to admit but the lack of affection is starting to get to me. Going to work is not an option right now, last time I tried was a disaster, but I've been trying to keep myself busy during the day as much as I can. Helping out Avery, even if she hasn't needed it. She's under the impression that Logan is madly in love with me, and I haven't had the heart to correct her. In the beginning, I thought I was going to lose my best friend because of what happened between me and Logan. So, the last thing I want to do is let her in on how he is behaving right now. She knows about Troj punching Logan, but I just played it down and made out as if Troj was exaggerating. The truth is, he wasn't exaggerating. Logan was starting to get aggressive with his affection and although I told him to stop, he didn't want to whilst I was in the club. I think Troj had had enough of Logan's behavior and hit him, hoping to straighten him out but it only made things worse. Not in a physical sense, Logan has never tried to hurt me, but in the way, he now doesn't want me to be at the club because of the trouble it caused. Well, that and the paparazzi. They have vilified me in the press and dragged me over the coals, but they don't know the truth, they only want to print stuff that helps them get the clicks online. I gave up caring about that one a while ago, if Logan wasn't going to acknowledge it, why should I?

In all honesty, spending this time with Ozzy has been incredible. I'm never going to make up for the fact he's lost his mother, but I will make damn sure that boy knows he is loved. Despite Logan's drinking in the evening, he has always been around in the day if we have needed him and although Ozzy spends most weekends with his grandparents, I make sure that we do things together every chance we get. Those are the moments I cherish, seeing Logan with his boy, completely relaxed and living in the moment rather than getting caught up with the demons in his mind. For the most part, Logan's drinking hasn't affected Ozzy at all, he just thinks that some days, Daddy has a bad head and needs to sleep for it to get better. He's already been through so much. It breaks my heart to think that he would worry about his Daddy being sick like his Mommy too. Hearing my phone vibrate in my bag, I pull over and see a message from Logan.

Can you grab me a bottle of Jack from the store? This one's empty.

The lack of please or thank you doesn't go unnoticed, but I also know that he only opened that bottle just before I got back, so it's safe to say that he's going to be wasted. This bodes well for me and the fact that I rejected him before I walked out. The amount of alcohol in his system will hopefully help him forget that and just help him believe that I will be back soon with more. As I pull off, I start my journey back home but not before running into the store to grab some milk and another bottle of Jack. My hope is that he is already asleep by the time I get back but the only way to know is if I stop putting off the inevitable and head back.

The drive around was very calming and just what I needed to help me to relax before facing Logan. I don't want to have to reject him again, but the smell of alcohol is really starting to get to me. I think it's my tolerance level reaching its peak and it's my body's way of letting me know I've had enough.

As I walk through the door, I'm greeted by silence. Looks like Logan has passed out in his bedroom. Putting everything away, I tiptoe towards Logan's room and that's when I know he isn't asleep. As I push open the door, I hear him in the shower singing to himself. He really does have a beautiful voice and it's at this moment I realize how much I've missed hearing it. Even when he is blind drunk, he can still hold a tune. Sitting on the edge of the bed, I listen and absorb the words he sings. None of it is making any sense but just hearing him is enough. The smell of his body wash is the next thing I have the pleasure of taking in. I'm normally out or busy when he has a shower and I now realize that I've deprived myself of this little privilege. Hearing him turn off the shower, I wait with anticipation as he exits the bathroom, surprising myself at how happy I am to see him considering how I felt when I walked through the door.

"Hey doll, you're back. I missed you." His speech is a little slurred and his eyes are glazed over, instantly pulling me back to the reality I'm living. Seeing him with wet hair, fresh from the shower was the sight I was waiting for, but what I wasn't banking on was just how drunk he would still be. I don't know why I thought it'd be any different, I knew how much he had to drink. I guess for a moment in time, I just wanted to believe that everything was different. Getting up, I make my way into the bathroom so I can get ready for bed. Cleaning up the chaos of the bathroom wasn't what I had planned but it's what I do regardless, eliminating any trace of drunken Logan. Slipping into my sleep shirt, an old Guilty Pleasure shirt that Logan gave me the first time I stayed over, I make my way back into the bedroom, ready to put this day to an end at long last. As I step out of the bathroom, I walk straight into Logan's chest but before I have a chance to say anything, his mouth is on mine. The alcohol tastes bitter on his tongue and makes my stomach turn but my core cries out for his touch, the same as always. My body's so conflicted that it makes my head spin. Pushing away from him, I try to catch my breath.

"Wow, Logan. Nothing like giving me a moment to get out of the bathroom." Looking up into his eyes, any resistance I tried putting up breaks down instantly. I see the loss he is trying to hide, the pain he is carrying on his shoulders, trying to be strong for everyone around him. Lunging at me again, his lips land on my neck as his hands make their way under my shirt. Stopping him once more, I step back to keep him at arm's length.

"What is it you want, Logan? Tell me what's going on in that head of yours?" Grabbing my face, he lifts it up and stares deep into my eyes,

"I just need you, doll. I need to be inside you." I would love to tell him no. Tell him that this isn't right, none of this is right. But I can't. Something inside of me comes alive whenever he is near and every time he tells me he needs me, something inside me breaks. A part of myself that I never knew existed until he brought it to life with nothing more than a simple touch.

This is wrong. I know he is using me to make himself feel better, but I can't stop him. Fearing that I may never feel his touch again, I give in to his temptation.

THIRTY-FOUR

LOGAN

S elfish
 /ˈsɛlfɪʃ/
 adjective
 (of a person, action, or motive) lacking consideration for other people; concerned chiefly with one's own personal profit or pleasure.

Selfish. Look up the word in the dictionary and I'm sure you'll see my face. I know what I'm doing is wrong, but how else can I show Melody just how much she means to me?! every time I talk, I say something wrong. I'm terrified of losing her, so I show her how much I care the only way I know how. She thinks I'm mourning the loss of Gabby, but that isn't what is happening. I'm mourning the loss of my son's mother, I know that he's gonna have to go the rest of his life, losing the one woman who would love him unconditionally. Being stuck with me isn't a life for anyone, let alone a kid. Some days I'm barely able to look after myself. Melody thinks that I only keep her around because of Ozzy, but again, she's wrong. Yes, Ozzy loves her SO much, Gabby told me he's loved her since the day he met her, and I can sympathize with that one. The only difference is, he tells her every day how much he loves her, more so since losing Gabby. I haven't even told her once. I can't. Everything I love turns to shit in the end.

She doesn't think that I feel her hesitation at night when I make my move, but I do. I just can't seem to bring myself to stop, she makes me feel alive. She makes me feel like the man I know I could be. The man I'm capable of being with the right people in my life, loving me for who I am and not what I can give them. I may not be perfect, but I am as close to perfect as I'll ever be when I'm with her.

I take all I can from her every night in the hope I'm not taking away from her beautiful self, but I see the way she lights up when I touch her. I would give up everything just to see that.

I'm stuck in a rut. Every day I wake up, telling myself this is the day that I won't have a drink, today is the day I finally show Melody what kind of man I can be, for her, but every day, something makes me reach for the bottle. I wouldn't say that I have a problem yet as I've seen firsthand what addiction looks like. Watching Eddie spiral until he hit rock bottom, I think scared everyone around him about addiction. He was a mess. All day, every day and he couldn't function until he knew where his next fix was coming from. The difference here is that I know I can function without the drink. I'm just enjoying the numbing that comes at the end of each bottle. I manage to stay sober the whole time my son is awake, so I know I'm okay.

Today is not a day I tell myself I won't be drinking though. Today is a day that I have invited the guys over to watch the game and share a beer together. This was actually Melody's idea and she got up early to prepare food for us all, before going off on the spa day that I got for her and Avery as a thank you for everything they've done. As soon as she leaves, I break out all the drinks I was storing in the garage. Today is gonna be messy so I have booked the full works for the girls, including an evening meal so that me and the boys can fully let loose. Everyone is due to arrive any minute, so I crack open a bottle of beer and start as I mean to go on. I do have to get Ozzy later from his grandparents but that is neither here nor there, he'll be straight off to bed by the time he's home. The bang on the door pulls me out of my head and Cody comes bursting through.

"What's up, mother lover?" We hug quickly as I hand him a drink.

"How's it going, man? Are the other guys behind you?" A strange look passes his face as he looks at the floor.

"Yeah, about that. I don't think anyone else is coming." Confusion mars my features as I think back to previous messages.

"They all said they'd be here. What the fuck?"

"I don't fucking know, man. Eddie said something about having Faith and Hunter said something about a bird he was banging. I don't know what's going on with Spencer. That dude's been off for a minute now. He was even talking about getting a tattoo yesterday. It's weird, he's never said anything like that before. He's always been a good, clean living type of guy. I mean, how many times have we taken the piss out of him, telling him to grow a pair?" Cody has a point, this does seem out of character for him, but the truth is, I don't have time to worry about anyone else, I have enough shit to deal with myself. Spencer not being here doesn't bother me as I'm still mad at him. The words he said to Melody still play on my mind and it's only because of her, I haven't said anything to him. She begged me to leave it, so I promised her I would. The other guys not showing up has pissed me off though and my beer is gone in the blink of an eye because of it. I said that I wouldn't get blind drunk today and when I spoke those words, I meant them but the guys not showing up makes my blood boil. So, fuck the world right now, I'm gonna do what I want.

"Hey Code, why don't you call around and invite a few more people over? Let's make a real party out of this. We're supposed to be rockstars for fucks sake." Quick as a flash, his phone is out of his pocket.

"I'm on it, dude."

Thirty minutes later and my house is full of people I don't know but the truth is, I couldn't be happier. Everyone is laughing and having a good time, and this is exactly what I needed to get out of this rut I've been stuck in. I forgot what it feels like to be a rock star, admired by everyone, and I've missed it. There is no better feeling in the world than knowing everyone in the room loves you. I see the looks some of the women are giving me, and however much I love it, I would never do anything to jeopardize what I have with Melody. Fuck knows where this thing is going with us, but I know she needs me as much as I do her. She doesn't think I hear her in the night, confessing her love for me but I hear every word spoken. I choose not to say it back because the truth is, I'm so messed up and confused right now that I don't know how I feel.

Today though, today I party like it's 1999 and make up for the time I lost when I was married.

THIRTY-FIVE

MELODY

Today is a day I've been looking forward to for ages. Logan has booked me and Avery into a spa as a thank you to both of us for everything we've done. It isn't until I walk through the doors of the swanky hotel we are booked into that I physically feel myself relax. This is going to be amazing. Avery is waiting at the reception for me already.

"About time, Dee, I feel like I've been waiting a lifetime for you." We hug as soon as I am close enough and I'm sure to give her an extra squeeze to let her know how much I miss her.

"As dramatic as ever, Ree." She bumps me with her hip as I check us both in. Logan has gone all out on this spa day and has booked us both in for the works. I'll be sure to thank him later in a way I know he'll appreciate. By the time I see him later, I will be relaxed and ready for anything.

Getting off the phone with Jenny and I can feel my blood boiling. This whole time I've been with Logan, I've always cut him some slack and picked up where he has been lacking. But this is the final straw. I have tried my best with everything I've done, being sure to be there for Ozzy, leaving Logan in a position where he doesn't have to worry about it, and on the one day I ask him to get Ozzy, he lets everyone down. We both knew that he would be having a drink today, but he promised me he wouldn't touch the Jack until Ozzy was in bed. I even left a note and set an alarm on his phone, telling him to book the uber so that he didn't have to drive. It's impossible to expect him not to drink on game day but never in a million years did I think he would forget to pick up his own son. Luckily enough Jenny is happy to keep him there tonight and drop him off at school in the morning. I'll just have to pick up his things when I have got over the embarrassment of all of this.

This is the first time since all of this started that I've finally managed to relax. With everything that's happened in these few short months, I feel like I have been walking around in a daze, waiting to wake up from the nightmare. If it wasn't for the touch of Logan's skin on mine, it would have been the worst few months of my life. He has been my light in all of the dark, but I think it's safe to say the fuse has finally blown. I make a promise to call Avery later as I leave the hotel, making it home in record time. The scene that awaits me as I walk through the door tips me over the very small edge I was already on. Bottles and food everywhere, as well as bodies of people whom I've never seen before. Making my way around the house a feeling of dread crawls up my spine as I stand outside his bedroom door. Knowing I'm not ready to deal with that just yet, I make my way back into the living room and get everyone to leave, not wanting to have any witnesses to my impending breakdown. I know how Logan and I got together wasn't the ideal start to any relationship, but after speaking to Gabriella and everyone that knew him, I never once worried about what he would get up to when I wasn't around. The fear that is wrapped around my heart is like nothing I've ever experienced before and hope never to feel it again. As the final stray leaves, I shut the door behind them and make my way back to the bedroom. Standing outside the door, I listen to see if I can hear any noises coming from inside but honestly, my heart is beating so fast that it's the only thing I hear right now. Taking one last deep breath, I turn the handle and push the door open. Much to my relief, the only thing I see is Logan passed out on the bed, fully clothed. The relief is short-lived though as the anger I felt earlier comes back with vengeance.

Going into the bathroom, I fill up a bucket full of water and make my way over to Logan, emptying the contents over his head.

"What the fuck?" His eyes finally meet mine after his initial panic. "What the hell, doll?" Turning on my heels, I make my way out of the bedroom. The living room won't clean itself, and I sure as hell ain't letting Ozzy come home to this so I might as well make a start as there is no chance I'll be going to sleep anytime soon. Also, Logan needs to change that bed before the wetness seeps through. I barely manage to get a bag out of the drawer before Logan catches up to me,

"What the fuck was that about Melody?" This is the first time in a long time that Logan has used my name. I've heard him say it when he's speaking to other people, but he hasn't used it to address me for months.

"Melody, are you listening to me? What the fuck did I do to deserve that?" The anger in his voice only enrages my own.

"What, you mean aside from this?" Pointing to the living room, his eyes follow the direction of my hand.

"It's just a bit of mess, Dee. I'll clean it up tomorrow." I think he believes that is it. He has completely forgotten the most important thing.

"Yeah, you're right Logan. Just a bit of mess, right? Nothing that can't be sorted." In his drunken state, he mistakes my sarcasm for humor as he steps towards me with his arms outstretched. "Where's Ozzy, Logan?" The words hit him like I hoped as he stops dead, dropping his arms. A moment of silence passes with him not saying anything, so I give him the answer to my own question. "He's still with Jenny and Des, thanks to your no show. They called me when you didn't arrive, so I dealt with it. What the Hell happened Logan?" I watch as a range of emotions cross his face and wait patiently for his reply. What I wasn't expecting was for his anger to be directed at me.

"Well, I'm sorry that I'm not as perfect as you. Maybe if you hadn't left me on my own today things would have been different?"

"Really, Logan? You're trying to blame me for this? Are you fucking kidding me? I went out for the day, at your insistence. I even told you no, as I wanted you to relax with the boys and have a good time, worry free. But you told me you'd already booked it, so I *had* to go. I set up every possible reminder I could have, so that you didn't forget. Honestly, I didn't think you would need so many reminders. I almost expected to get a message from you, telling me that you don't know what I was so worried about. I thought I'd come home, and we'd laugh about how many alarms I set up on your phone. Where the fuck is your phone and how did you manage to miss them? I don't understand, Ozzy is the most important thing in the world, and you let him down tonight, Logan." The words sting as they leave my mouth. I never wanted to hurt Logan, but I have reached my breaking point. He needs to know just how much he's let everyone down.

"What gives you the fucking right to talk about my son? You know nothing. You waltz in here like you fucking own the place. Trying to erase the memories we both have of his mother…"

"Don't you dare say that Logan. I have never tried to erase

anything. All I've ever wanted to do was look after you both, make sure you..."

"I don't need looking after, Melody. All I ever needed was a warm place to stick my dick. And guess what darling, you were it."

"You don't mean that. I know you don't mean that. You're just angry and drunk." The sadistic smile that spreads across his face is unlike anything I've ever seen.

"Is that what you think? I hate to break it to you, doll, but you would never replace Gabby. She was a once in a lifetime kind of thing."

He turns and leaves as the impact of his words settles in. I must stand here for thirty minutes or more, not knowing what to do with myself. The only thing I do know is that I can't be here, I need to leave. Rushing into the bedroom, I hope that Logan is passed out so that I can pack a small bag and go without interruption. Much to my relief, Logan isn't even in his room as I open the door. Peaking my head around, I can see him passed out on Gabriella's bed, sleeping as if none of this just happened. Today has certainly been eventful with many discoveries along the way. But as I sit here, on the floor, I know there is no coming back from it. So, I do the only thing I can. I pack up everything I own and vow never to step foot in here ever again.

THIRTY-SIX

LOGAN

6 months later.

I've spent the past six months looking for her. Six months of searching but never finding her. I fucked up big time that fateful night six months ago and I've regretted it ever since. I fucked up again when I told Avery everything that happened, as I thought Melody would've told her. Turns out, women don't always share everything. I don't know why Melody didn't tell her but what I do know is that it took me a very long time to get Avery back on my side. But even now I know I'm walking a tightrope with her. She's the only link I have left to Melody.

She upped and left with my horrific words going around her head, thinking what I said was true and I've done everything in my power to find her and let her know how I really feel. The truth is, I was hurting, and it was like I wanted to drag her down with me. I should've known that she was too strong to stand there and tolerate my bullshit. The one thing I have learned though is that life goes on and no matter what I try and do to slow it down, the clock keeps ticking. I lost my mojo for a while there but losing Melody has given me the inspiration I needed to find myself again. I've been in the recording studio, trying to heal my heart as much as I can by pouring out the pain into the music. The feedback we've had so far has been amazing and the record label are loving it. But I know I'm headed into a shit storm now because I did an interview recently that I was asked not to do, and it's airing shortly. That was most likely the reason for the phone call from Belinda, demanding I get to the office as soon as possible. Fingers crossed that Avery can help me out, again.

Every time I knock on the door, I feel a nervousness I can't explain. In such a short amount of time, a lot happened here and the memories of her are strong.

"Oh, it's you." The smile drops from Avery's face as soon as she lays eyes on me.

"Hey, is there any chance you could have Oz for a few hours please? I can take him with me if you can't but it's always nicer for him to spend time with Zach if he can."

"Got nothing to do with the fact that you wanted to try and catch me out? Hoping you'd see Melody here?" biting my lip, I try my hardest not to smile. Avery may not like me very much, but she knows me pretty well. I thank God every day for my little boy, now more than ever. Avery wanted to string me up when Melody left. She blamed me for everything, and I hate to say it, but she isn't wrong with that one. It is a hundred percent my fault that Melody left, and I miss her every day. It was a bit rough for everyone in the beginning. I'd love to tell you that as soon as she left, I pulled myself together straight away, but that would be a boldfaced lie. It took me three months and losing my son, to his grandparents, to get me out of that hole. Avery has also been worth her weight in gold through it all and she knows this, as I tell her all the time. I don't know why she even bothered with me? I destroyed her best friend, tearing her apart with words that will burn at my soul for as long as I live. I single-handedly took away the life that Avery and Melody had built for themselves, yet she still lets me in her life, looking after my boy whenever she can. Before she has a chance to reply to my question, Ozzy goes running into the house to find Zach. "Shall I take that as a yes, you will have him?" I give her the biggest smile possible.

"Damn you, Logan, you know I'll always have him. Did you also know that it's six months to the day that you chased my best friend away from me?" The guilt trip is horrible, but I let her give it, whilst I hang my head in shame.

"I know. And I also know that sorry will never be enough but if you tell me where she is, I can at least try and make it up to her. Even if she doesn't want to be with me, I want her here with you. Just give me the chance to make things right, Ree. Even if it takes the rest of my days to do it, I will. I'll give you both whatever you need to heal and move on." The sympathy that flashes in Avery's eyes isn't missed by me. She knows how I feel but Melody made a decision and she's sticking to it.

"She had her reasons, Logan. Whereas I don't agree with them, it isn't my fight, so I have to respect her decision to leave."

"What does Barry think of it all?"

"Barry is living his best life right now. Since that franchise with the Biker boys went through, business is booming." Turns out the biker I had a run-in with really was just trying to help. They bought out the Cherry Pickers brand, to use on some of their existing clubs, but left Barry with a top role in the franchise.

"Anyway, I gotta shoot, emergency meeting at the record label. I'll message you when I'm on my way back, okay?"

"Don't worry about it, I'll drop him off with you tomorrow. Zach will love it if Ozzy stays over."

"What would I do without you, Avery?" I flash her another

winning smile as I turn to leave but before I make it to the car, she shouts over.

"That shit doesn't work on me Logan. Save it for some other sap." Since Avery has gotten to know that biker, Troj, her interests seem to have changed. I don't know if anything is going on between the two, but I do know she spends time with him every time he's in town. I've even seen his bike outside her house on a few occasions, but it isn't my place to get involved so I just leave her to it.

The drive to the city went a lot quicker than I would've liked and before I know it, I'm bracing myself as I enter the office. I'm surprised to be greeted by the rest of the band as I open the door because I thought this was a meeting to give me a shit about the interview. I asked them to leave it as long as possible before sending a copy to our manager as there was a chance he may pull it, insisting they don't air it. It may be a done deal as far as I'm concerned but it's amazing what the label can do if they really want to, like making interviews disappear.

"Here he is, the man of the hour." Hunter announces as I make my way in and take a seat. Spencer shoots me a dirty look before turning to talk to Hunter.

"Why are we here? This is ridiculous. Logan fucks up again, but we all suffer for it." He's been in a dark place ever since Gabby died but none of us are sure why as he doesn't open up to any of us anymore. He tends to get angry with me and I let him, better to get mad at me than anyone else. Looking over to Eddie, I give him a nod. I haven't said anything to anyone about the interview as I know they would've tried to stop me, so this is all on me. The management asked me not to speak about my problems on TV again as they feel it's pushing away our fans. Apparently, everyone is sick to death of me talking about the one that got away. Ronald, our manager for the last six years, comes storming in with Belinda struggling to keep up behind him. She's yet to be a part of a good telling off at the hands of the mighty Mr. Berry, so that'll be a new experience for her. Cody sits bolt upright as soon as he spots Belinda, ready to play his new favorite game of let's see how quickly we can make her blush.

"Princess Belle, how are you, beautiful?" And there she goes already, dropping her notes in horror. After she picks everything up, and with a few f-bombs from Ron, they both take a seat at the table. Eyes straight on me.

"You know what I'm going to say right, Logan? This shit seriously has to stop. What person in their right mind wants their favorite rock star balling on TV about a girl? That shit is airing right now and there is fuck all I can do to stop it. But you already knew that didn't you?"

"Yes Ronald. I asked them not to send it to you until the very last minute otherwise they would lose their exclusive. You may not like what I'm doing or what I'm going through, but this is my life. I kept quiet for years about who I am but no more. No more hiding away in the dark, unable to voice how I feel or who I love, just to keep the label happy."

"If it wasn't for this fucking label, you would have nothing. You would be nothing." Everyone's mouth drops open at the words that spew out of his mouth. If we ever needed an example about how we are simply a cog in the big wheel, this was it.

"Fuck you, Ron." I rise from my seat and Belinda speaks up for the first time ever.

"That's enough. No one needs to speak to anyone else like that, I won't have it." Cody looks on in awe, unable to take his eyes off her.

"Well said Bells, you tell 'em." Ronald swiftly turns her anger towards her.

"Who the fuck do you think you are? I'll talk to these pieces of shit however the fuck I want. I'm the one in charge here, so you all…" He doesn't get a chance to finish that sentence as Cody jumps across the table and knocks him clean out.

"Sorry you had to see that Bells, but he was not getting away with talking to you like that." Belinda looks on in shock but bounces back quickly.

"I guess I need to add 'find a new manager' to the agenda then?" And just like that, she calls security and has Ronald taken away.

I was sure that this would have us all sued. Or fired, but she assured us otherwise. This is the first time that any of us have seen this side of him but apparently this type of behavior is normal around the office and everyone's had enough of it. He was already on his last warning and this was just the push they needed. This would also explain why he went through so many assistants but as she has now proved to us, Belinda is the best.

"I need to get a drink. This has been more than enough excitement for one day." Before anyone can say a word, I am out of my chair and leaving the room, ignoring the concerned calls for me to stay. The interview that I recorded would be nearly finished by now and the thought of it being out in the world, for Melody to see makes me need a drink more than ever. And knowing that Ozzy is with Avery until tomorrow makes the decision all too easy.

THIRTY-SEVEN

MELODY

The past six months have been a struggle, I'm not gonna lie. Getting over Logan has been one of the hardest things I've ever had to do. Especially on days like today when it seems he's everywhere I turn. The band dropped a new album six weeks ago, so they have been doing loads of radio interviews, magazine articles, and TV appearances. Even the coffee shop I'm working in has been using promotional coasters with the band's picture on. So, my only escape is my day off, providing I don't watch the TV, read the latest gossip magazine or go online.

Wiping down the table that's just been vacated, I swipe the stained coasters into the bin, getting the same twisted satisfaction that I did the first time I did it. It's not Logan's fault completely that we went so wrong. The timing was terrible. He needed time to get over losing his wife. He said he didn't love her like that and although I do believe him, he still needed time to grieve. He needed time to mourn the loss of his friend, his former lover, the mother of his son. I should've walked away the moment he told me he needed me but the trouble with Logan is that he makes me weak. I've never considered myself to be a weak person, but Logan broke me down in ways no one has ever done before. Hearing him say he needs me had me running to him as fast as I could. The best thing I did though was walk away. We were not good for one another at that moment in time and his words hurt me. Things may have felt good, especially the amazing sex, but we were always gonna end this way. He was never going to heal whilst I was around picking up all the pieces for him.

The bell over the door snaps me out of memories as another happy customer leaves with a coffee in hand, ready for the rush hour traffic home. Meghan, my co-worker, sweeps up behind me, hurrying me along.

"Chasing me with the broom isn't gonna make your shift end any sooner, ya know!"

"I know, I just want to get out on time later so the more I do now, the less I have to do then." Can't argue with her on that one. "Also, I have a date with Chad later. I mean, he's no Guilty Pleasure but he'll do I guess" she says, shrugging her shoulder with a glint in her eye. That reference was no accident. I found out not long after meeting Meghan that she is obsessed with the band. I haven't dared tell her that Logan is the ex I've been avoiding, she'd freak. I try to change the subject with a question I know she hates.

"When are you gonna meet a decent guy and settle down?" Meghan looks like someone just walked across her grave. That shudder was real.

"I'll tell you what Dee, I'll settle down the moment Logan pierce walks through that door and pulls out a ring." The mention of his name sends a chill down my spine and settles in the most inappropriate place. The bell rings above the door and me and Meghan look at each other before averting our eyes towards the guy who just entered. Meghan looks almost disappointed that it isn't Logan, down on one knee just for her. We both laugh as I head back behind the counter to serve the man who just walked in. The counters in this place are ridiculously high, with a small counter on the end for people to collect their drink if they can't reach up and get it. Just as I'm finishing up, I hear Meghan squealing as she dashes behind the counter, scooping up the TV remote. As I glance over towards the TV, I see Logan looking back at me which causes me to freeze.

"Dee, come take a seat and watch how a real man acts." If only she knew. Ignoring her, I carry on cleaning the counter. All whilst trying to block out the familiar voice on the TV, trying to tell me how much he misses the love that got away. The stab in my chest is real as I fight back the tears, praying that it's over soon.

It wasn't soon enough but that doesn't matter. I know if he's only on the TV for seconds, I would still have to listen to Meghan as she harps on about it, over and over again. Even though they have been shoved down everyone's throats lately, I've managed to avoid listening to what Logan has said, although Meghan has great pleasure filling me in, every time. It doesn't hurt so much coming from her, but I still manage to block her out as much as I can. This is going to be torture.

"Oh Dee, did you hear him?"

"Well, I tried not to." She scowls at my words as she continues.

"Who in their right mind would walk away from that? I mean, he is everything you could want in a man." Trying my hardest not to get annoyed, I answer the calmest way I can.

"At the end of the day, you don't know this man. For all you know he could be a nightmare to live with. He may come across as lovely and warm but inside he might be cold and damaged. You just don't know Megs." The dreamy look in her eyes tells me that she didn't listen to a word I said. Ignorance is bliss when you don't know any better.

"But Dee, don't you feel anything when he sings about his

Sweet, Sweet Melody? I mean, that's your name! I think my ovaries would explode if I heard him singing about me like that." If only she knew, "Well, whoever this crazy lady is, I hope she's happy with herself and the choices she made." Am I happy with the choices I made? Yes and no. I made the right choice for me at the time, but I miss my friend. I know I did the right thing for everyone involved, including Logan. Rather than respond, I busy myself behind the counter, cleaning the imaginary dirt I've already cleaned. The bell rings above the door again as the lingering customer makes her way out, probably fed up with hearing about Logan fucking Pierce by now.

The sound of glass shattering against the floor breaks the silence and as I look over to Meghan, she is frozen to the spot. Confused by what's happened I scan around the room and that's when everything stops.

"Melody?" My name out of his mouth with his eyes solely focused on me has me stunned silent. I don't know what to say as he eagerly awaits my reply. My mouth opens and closes, yet no words follow. "Is it really you, doll?" I nod, not trusting any words that will leave my lips. The tension in the air is thick and my heart is beating at a frantic pace.

"Holy fucking shit. Logan Pierce, he's the ex you ran away from? You're Sweet Melody? Omg my head is spinning. This is too much." Raising her hand to her head, she leans against the counter as I'm sure every conversation we've ever had about Guilty Pleasure flashes through her mind.

"I'm sorry, Megs." Tears start to cloud my vision as I squeak out the words that hurt us both.

"Dee, you've gone a funny color." Meghan rushes behind the counter and helps me over to a seat and Logan watches in stunned silence. Meghan grabs me a bottle of water as Logan stares at me, in shock.

"When were you gonna tell me, doll?" The hurt in his voice

cuts through me like a sharp knife and I almost forget that Meghan is here.

"Tell him what Dee? Are you telling me he didn't know?" The sharpness of her words has me wincing away, trying to shield myself from the upset I know is going to follow. With Meghan's and Logan's eyes both on me, I say the words I've avoided saying for the past seven months.

"Logan, I'm pregnant."

THIRTY-EIGHT

LOGAN

The words echo around my mind.

"I'm pregnant."

Every emotion hits me at the same time.

Anger.

Joy.

Happiness.

Confusion.

Sadness at the fact she felt she had to run away and not share this with me. Grabbing a seat and pulling it to sit in front of her, I take her hand in mine.

"Why didn't you tell me, doll? Why didn't anyone tell me? I can't believe you've been doing this on your own." I want to ask a million more questions, but I can see the fear in her eyes as she watches me. As I sit and look at her, I can see how pale she is too.

"I couldn't tell you, Logan." The words cut me deep as they leave her mouth, "You weren't ready. Gabriella told me the only reason you stayed with her was because she got pregnant, and I didn't want to do that to you again. I didn't want you to be stuck with me because I wasn't careful enough and got caught pregnant, and I wasn't getting rid of it, Logan." I struggle to get a handle on everything that's happening, but I know that I'd never have felt like I was stuck with her. Without her even knowing it, she is my everything.

"First of all, I would never have asked you to get rid of my baby. Second, I would never have felt stuck with you. I'm sorry I got myself into such a mess. You leaving me was the worst thing that happened but it also helped me realize just how much of a mess I was. This past six months have been fucking awful without you, but it was exactly what I needed to get my shit in order." Stopping to take a breath, I give her a moment to digest what I'm saying. The relief I feel just by seeing her is amazing. Touching her hand, finally having the skin-to-skin contact that I've been craving is worth more than all the money in the world. This moment makes me realize that I'd give everything up for her. Fame and fortune mean nothing without her.

"You're not mad at me?"

"No, doll. I'm not mad. I'm angry at myself that I pushed you to a place where you didn't think you could share this with me though."

The thought of her having come this far on her own is nearly my undoing but I know now isn't the time for self-pity. This just proves something that I already knew. Melody is the strongest, most selfless person I've ever met. The fact that she knows I have money and yet she still did this alone. Working in a shitty coffee shop to provide for my baby. The baby that I didn't know about until five minutes ago. I'm so wrapped up in my thoughts that I don't see the tears rolling from her eyes. It's not until she speaks and the crack in her voice gives it away.

"I'm sorry Logan. I Just..." Not letting her finish her sentence, I wrap her up in my arms, finally. Something as simple as smelling her hair is the remedy I needed to feel whole again.

"Don't apologize, Melody. Just, come home with me." I release her slightly, so I can look into her beautiful eyes. "Me and Ozzy want you back." Everything inside me wants to tell her that I need her, but I don't want to put that pressure on her. She needs to know she's wanted, not needed. Any decision she makes needs to be her own but honestly, I can't see myself walking out of this place without her. The world slows down a little as I hold my breath, waiting for her to answer. I have more questions, but I can't go on without the answer to this one. Just as she opens her mouth, the bell above the door chimes, and the silence is broken. Not only by the bell but by Meghan's screaming. I completely forgot she was here.

"We're closed, get out." she screams at the poor person who dared to want a coffee.

"Logan, what are you doing... Dee, is that you? Holy shit, you've got really fat since I last saw you." Hunter is lucky as Melody lets out a laugh, standing up to hug him.

"Oh Hunter, I'm seven months pregnant, and I've missed you like crazy." Taking a step back from her, Hunter doesn't release Melody as he asks.

"It's not mine, is it?" He smirks and he has a glint in his eye. This is the reason why he always ends up in so much trouble.

"Hunter, don't say stupid shit to my girl." Eyebrows raise on both of them as they stare at me.

"Last time I checked dude, she wasn't your girl." Everything in me wants to punch him in the face right now but he does have a point. Not willing to wait any longer, I ready myself to ask the other question I had for her.

Pulling my wallet from my back pocket, I drop down on one knee and pull out the ring I've been carrying around with me since she left.

"Will you marry me, doll?"

"Logan, what are you doing? You don't have to do this, you know. Just because I'm pregnant doesn't mean... Wait, where did you get that ring?" The confused look on her face would be cute if I wasn't desperate for an answer.

"I've been carrying this with me everywhere in the hope that I'd have the chance to ask you. It was a reminder that I needed to get myself right, for you. It's you, Melody Grace. It's always been you. You don't need to understand but I do need you to agree to be my wife, so, what do you say?"

"I just, this is a lot to take in…"

"For the love of God, Melody, will you say yes already," Meghan shouts from the side, and as we both look toward her. Hunter is on her in a second, dragging her out the back despite her attempts at protesting.

"Yes."

It's a small, simple word, but it's just changed my life.

"Say that again."

"Yes Mr. Pierce, I will marry you." I push the ring onto her finger and jump to my feet, picking her up and having her back where she belongs, in my arms.

"I love you so much, Melody." Hearing a sob from her has me placing her back down, worried that I've hurt her or the baby.

"You've never told me that before when you're sober." Guilt scratches at my heart but I knew this wouldn't be guilt-free.

"Well, get used to it as I plan on telling you every day for the rest of my life."

My lips finally land on hers and all is right in the world again. This is where I am meant to be. Wrapped in the arms of the woman who I love more than life itself. I loved Gabby for giving me my son, but I wasn't in love with her. My feelings for Melody proved that. Gabby deserved better than me but at least I made sure that she was as happy as she could be in her final days. Avery told me what Gabby said to Melody, and knowing she gave Melody her blessing means more to me than words could ever say. Not once did she make either of us feel bad for the way we felt, proving once more what a special woman she was. It's weird sometimes, where life takes you, but I truly believe that me and Melody were written in the stars. I've never been a big believer in fate but how could I argue it now? What are the chances of me and Melody finding each other the way we did? It may not have been ideal but in all honesty, I wouldn't change it for anything. Now all I need to do is get her home and make an honest woman out of her, forever.

EPILOGUE

MELODY

3 months later

As I sit her with my one-month-old baby girl wrapped up in my arms, I can't help but reflect back on the last few months.

I didn't lie when I said I wouldn't step foot back in Gabriella's house. I didn't make Logan sell it, but I did tell him that I wouldn't go back there. That was Gabriella's family home, and it didn't feel right stepping foot back inside with everything that happened. With her and with Logan's parting words.

Kudos to him though, he got us another house in no time at all and we stayed with Avery while we waited for the sale to go through. It was as chaotic as you'd expect but I loved every second of it. I had not only my best friend and love of my life with me but the 2 kids I love with everything I am. I missed those boys so much it actually hurt me, so I soaked up every second I could with them both until Logan had the new house sorted. With the baby on the way, I wanted to make as much time for the boys because I knew everything would change as soon as she came along.

What Logan didn't tell me is that he bought the house across the street from us for Avery and Zach. She refused it at first, not wanting to take advantage of the fact he has money. But when Logan explained to her that he was doing it for me, she couldn't refuse. He told her after that he already signed it in her name, so it was hers whether she agreed or not.

We applied for our marriage license as soon as we got back, and we received it a month later. It all felt a bit rushed for me and I didn't want Logan to do it just because of the baby. So, we decided to let it expire, since it only lasts for 30 days. He'd been married pretty much his whole adult life so far, and I didn't want him feeling like he had to get married again. He was a bit upset at first as he said he wanted our baby girl to come into the world with us all together but after we had a talk, I made him realize that the most important thing is love. She would be coming into this world surrounded by love and that's all that mattered.

That was until day 28 of the marriage license. I had a total meltdown and freaked out about everything. I was only days away from my due date and the thought of not being married freaked me out.

So, Logan got us down to city hall and we were married on day 29 of our license with Avery, Eddie, and the boys as our only guests. Logan promised me a 'proper' wedding on our one-year anniversary, but this is everything I could have ever wanted. I've never been one for the fuss and fanfare of a big wedding, so this suited me perfectly.

Sure enough, baby girl came 3 days later and completed our beautiful family. We joked about me going into labour when we were at city hall, but thankfully that never happened.

Lyric Avery Pierce has changed our lives in a way none of us thought possible. She is an amazing baby who has her Daddy's calm, charming ways. She hypnotizes you with her beautiful blue eyes and has a touch of red in her hair that she gets from me. She is the perfect balance of me and Logan and despite the bumps along the way, she was conceived and born in love.

Things with the record label have slowed down a bit for Logan. He told me about his manager being sacked the day he found me, so they all decided to have a break. They have been constantly on the go for five years now and they are all starting to feel it. The timing wasn't great, with the release of a new album but Belinda insisted they take some time off as soon as she heard about everything that Logan has been through.

Eddie is with us every day as most of his family are in England. He has an apartment in the city, but he stays here most of the time. I fixed up the spare bedroom and turned it into his own little place so that he never feels like he has to leave. This would probably be weird for most newlyweds but let's be honest, nothing has ever been normal with me and Logan. Eddie isn't a man of many words, but he loves being surrounded by people. He may not join in as much as I'd like but he is a true people watcher. His addictions of the past still haunt him, so I think he likes to feel he's not alone.

We've not seen much of Cody and Hunter as they decided to use this time to travel to all the places they haven't visited. We do get regular updates via email though and normally a new picture of the latest local offerings. Which normally consists of a different woman each time.

Meghan pops over every now and again. Turns out her and Hunter had a little fling just before he went off on his travels. She handled that a lot better than I was expecting. I thought she'd have a meltdown, but she handed him a bag of condoms and wished him safe travels.

I don't even know where to start with Spencer. As soon as I was back, he reached out to me and Logan didn't like it. After talking about it, Logan soon realized that I was the only person that Spencer was speaking to. So, he let it go. Despite his own issues, he could see that Spencer needed someone and for some reason, that someone was me. Maybe it's because I'm an outsider or maybe it's just because I was there at the right time. Whatever it is, I've told Logan that I wasn't willing to ignore him in his time of need and he understood. He may not trust Spencer's intentions but he sure as hell trusts mine.

It's safe to say that Spencer has a dark cloud over him right now. The death of Gabriella hit him hard. He's picked up a new addiction, but thankfully, it's nothing like Eddie's. He's started getting tattoos. He seems to have a new one every time I see him. He asked all the boys to go and have one with him but so far, they've all said no.

It still feels weird not living with Avery and Zach but the fact they live over the street is the Godsend that Logan knew I needed. To be honest, they're here so much that it almost feels like we still live together. She's over here all the time with Ozzy, soaking up as much as she can of baby Lyric and helping me with everything I could need.

This past year has been a crazy one, to say the least. We've all suffered the loss of a great woman who connected us. Her blessing lives in my heart every day and I'm thankful for the time I had with her. Both as a friend and in her final days.

Although this isn't the life I imagined having, I wouldn't change a single thing. I have my best friend with me still, my baby girl who fills my heart in a way I never knew existed, and a man who would walk through Hell and high water to make sure his family is safe. This isn't a Disney fairy-tale, but the end is just the same.

Love wins every time.

ACKNOWLEDGMENTS

First and foremost, the biggest thanks I owe is to Emma, my BBB (Best Book Bish). This would never have been finished if it wasn't for you. I'd love to say you pushed me but we both know that isn't true because I wouldn't let you haha. But, this book wouldn't be what it is if it wasn't for you. Your support has been truly unbelievable, you are a total Universal Treasure.

Secondly, I'd love to thank Gela. Not only are you my best friend but you have been my biggest cheerleader. Your support in all aspects of my life is priceless and I love you. (This one's for David and Mother, I miss them).

Cassie Wildman, this story wouldn't have happened without you, literally. You helped me bring Logan and Melody to life. Without your support in the beginning, I may never have taken it any further. I love you Wildman.

My Ma and Pa, Although Pa might not see this as I've banned him from reading the book. Your support of me has been above and beyond, my whole life. I wouldn't be me, without you. I love you both more than words could ever say.

My Billie Babe. You have been the best writing buddy a girl could ask for. I didn't plan on my desk being your bed, but it was the best thing ever. You helped me push through when I needed someone to talk to. I will be sure to get you some catnip as a special thank you, just don't tell the others.

Brenda O Willis, Thank you for beta reading my baby, your feedback was hugely appreciated as you were the first person to read this book who had no emotional link to me.

Our Duchess, Anne Woolgar, Your blind faith in me and Emma hasn't gone unnoticed. It's amazing the people you meet at book signings. I love you, and Ade.

Sarah Goodman, you are a legend. I'm so glad I found you and I can't wait to actually meet you.

Kerry Heavens, thank you for bringing Logan to life and making him look as good as he deserves.

You, the reader, thank you for taking the time to read Logan and Melody's story. It was a bit touch and go at times, but I really appreciate you taking the time to love them as much as I do. Thank you for putting your faith in me.

My babies, Bungle, Loubs and Bubba. I love you 3 more than you can ever imagine, and it is a joy being your Mum. You 3 will always be my best achievements.

Last but by no means least, My husband, Si. You inspire me every day with the things you do (@sjpwrestlingpod) and it's about time people started to see and hear just how great you really are. Thank you for "making" me watch sweaty men in pants. You're a prick… But, you're my prick.

PLAYLIST

PLAYLIST FOR SWEET MELODY ON SPOTIFY

Thirty Seconds To Mars ~ Stay
Sixx A.M. ~ Smile
Chris Cornell ~ Patience
Ciara & Justin ~ Love Sex Magic
Extreme ~ More than words
Thirty Second To Mars ~ A Beautiful Lie
Sixx A.M ~ Sure feels right
Motley Crue ~ Girls Girls Girls
Heavens Basement ~ Nothing left to lose
Thirty Seconds To Mars ~ Love is madness
Velvet Revolver ~ Fall to pieces
Slash ft. Myles Kennedy ~ Battleground
Buckcherry ~ Sorry
Hinder ~ Shoulda
Slash ft. Fergie ~ Beautiful Dangerous
Pop Evil ~ Torn To Pieces
Thunder ~ Love walked in

I am a huge lover of music and I truly believe that music feeds my soul. The playlist above gives you an idea of where I was whilst I was writing Logan and Melody's story. The great thing about music is that it doesn't have to be the song as a whole that strikes a chord with you. Sometimes, a simple line can mean everything. If you ever hear a song that makes you think of my characters or their story, please reach out to me, I'd love to get your take.

Printed in Great Britain
by Amazon

62182963R00135